*a*re you using the chain shank on Shafir?" Taylor asked.

"Does anyone else hear mosquitoes buzzing?" Plum asked.

Taylor's face reddened with anger. She felt responsible for Shafir. It was Taylor who'd persuaded Plum that Shafir was a great horse for her to lease. She'd acted out of sheer desperation because Plum was about to lease Prince Albert.

Taylor would not let that happen to Prince Albert. It was a matter of life and death.

Ride over to
WILDWOOD STABLES

Good

Book

Luv
it

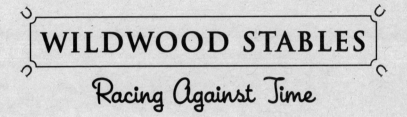

WILDWOOD STABLES
Racing Against Time

BY SUZANNE WEYN

SCHOLASTIC INC.
New York   Toronto   London   Auckland
Sydney   Mexico City   New Delhi   Hong Kong

ISBN 978-0-545-14981-5

12 11 10 9 8 7 6 5 4 3 2 1   10 11 12 13 14 15/0

Printed in the U.S.A.   40
First printing, May 2010

For *Amanda Maciel* with thanks for all her tender loving care in guiding this series with such cheerfulness and creativity, and for making it such fun to write.

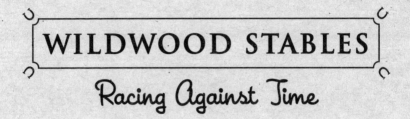

WILDWOOD STABLES

Racing Against Time

Chapter 1

$\mathcal{L}$eaning forward in her saddle, Taylor Henry focused between the ears of her black horse. He was loping along at a good, even clip. She and Prince Albert were moving together with a smoothness that made Taylor feel as if they had melded into one fantastical creature — a slim thirteen-year-old girl in jeans and a sweatshirt, her brown ponytail flying beneath a black helmet, magically merged with a powerful quarter horse gelding.

They were going pretty fast. Did she dare to go faster? To gallop?

How she longed to!

But she was nervous.

The rolling hills in the pasture behind Wildwood Stables were still green. October was holding fast to the last of summer's warmth, though the surrounding woods brimmed with orange, red, and yellow leaves. The gloriousness of the day, with its robin's egg–colored sky and cotton ball clouds, filled Taylor with a spirited daring.

A quick glance over her shoulder told Taylor that Pixie — the cream Shetland pony, with a matching wild, frazzled mane — was watching them as she grazed several yards away. As long as Pixie's friend, Prince Albert, stayed in sight, the small pony was content.

Taylor rose from the saddle, squeezing Prince Albert's sides tight with her thighs and knees, and got into two-point position, legs straight with her body balanced above the saddle.

Was she steady enough to gallop?

Taylor kept going, holding the two-point position. Before long, a quiver began in Taylor's knees. Her calf muscles burned with fatigue from holding herself upright.

Involuntarily, Taylor's upper body drifted left. She righted herself, using all her abdominal strength.

No, Taylor decided, sitting back down in the saddle. She wasn't confident she had the strength or balance to control Prince Albert if he was going any faster.

Before Taylor could fully experience her disappointment in her own riding ability, a teenage girl appeared in the pasture on a speckled gray. The horse was a mixed-breed mare, part barb and part quarter horse; a bit thick-bodied, with perky, high ears and a lush black mane and tail.

Daphne Chang rode toward Taylor with the graceful ease that marked her as an expert horsewoman. Daphne slowed her horse, Mandy, beside Taylor and Prince Albert. "Hi, Taylor. How come you're here on a Sunday? I thought Mondays, Wednesdays, and Fridays were the days you worked."

"I've decided to come at least one day every weekend from now on. I don't like Prince Albert and Pixie to be shut up in their stalls all that time between Friday and Monday."

"You should have called me. I would have turned them out in the pasture for you."

"Thanks, but I don't mind," Taylor said. "I like riding Prince Albert."

"You shouldn't be out here by yourself," Daphne chided mildly. "If you fell, who would know you needed help?"

"I came early. No one else was around to ride with," Taylor explained.

"Do you have your cell phone with you, at least?"

Taylor patted the phone in her back jeans pocket. "Yes! Besides, Prince Albert isn't going to throw me. He's the most steady, gentle guy in the world, aren't you, boy?"

"Even so," Daphne insisted. "You shouldn't go off alone like that."

"I guess not," Taylor allowed. She decided not to admit that she'd been about to attempt a gallop — a move that would have made her chances of falling pretty high, gentle horse or no. She was suddenly glad she'd thought better of it.

The girls rode together, their horses side by side, across the dandelion-strewn pasture. Pixie trotted up to join them and fell into step beside Prince Albert.

"The place is looking good, isn't it?" Taylor said to Daphne.

"Really good," Daphne agreed, "especially when you remember what a mess it was to start with."

The once thriving Wildwood Stables had been closed for many years, its wooden buildings and fences left to splinter and rot, until the current owner, Bernice LeFleur, inherited it. Taylor had had a part in convincing Mrs. LeFleur not to sell the place but to reopen it. It was part of the reason Taylor felt so deeply connected to Wildwood Stables.

The fact that Mrs. LeFleur opened the ranch and agreed to let Pixie and Prince Albert board there was, in Taylor's opinion, practically a miracle. Taylor had acquired the horse and pony in a rescue after they'd been abandoned by their owners. In exchange for Taylor's agreement to work at Wildwood three days a week and to let the ranch use Prince Albert and Pixie for lessons and trail rides, Mrs. LeFleur would pick up the expense of their food, vet care, and board. If Mrs. LeFleur hadn't made this generous arrangement, Taylor would never have had the money to keep Pixie and Prince Albert.

There was a problem, though.

In the month since Taylor had owned Prince Albert, she and the horse had formed an intense bond that Taylor cherished. The drawback to the deep and obvious love Prince Albert held for Taylor was that he wouldn't let anyone else ride him. Prince Albert needed to be a school horse that could take on the riders who would come to Wildwood Stables for lessons. He couldn't afford to be a one-girl horse.

Mrs. LeFleur was on a tight budget — she'd exhausted most of her money fixing up the ranch — so if she couldn't use Prince Albert for lessons, then she couldn't keep him. And if Mrs. LeFleur couldn't keep him, Taylor couldn't keep him on her own, either.

At a walking gait, the girls rode the horses toward the pasture fence. Taylor admired the way Daphne could unlatch the pasture fence, ride through, and then relatch it without getting down off Mandy. "You have to show me how to do that," she said to Daphne.

"I will," the older girl replied. "When are you going to let me teach you to ride English style?"

"I don't know. I've only ever ridden Western. I'm comfortable with it."

"You want to learn to jump, don't you? Jumping is only in English."

"You're right. I do want to jump," Taylor admitted.

As they rode down the slope leading from the pasture, the girls walked their horses past the large, fenced paddock with several outbuildings and storage sheds right behind it. Ahead of them was the main building, which housed the ranch's office, the tack room, and the stables, six indoor and six outdoor box stalls. In front of the main building was a round corral; on its right was another paddock.

Taylor's eyes narrowed as she realized there was a girl with long blonde hair in the corral, leading a chestnut Arabian mare with a white blaze down its muzzle. "I can't believe Plum's here already," Taylor muttered darkly. "I hope she doesn't think she's going to ride Shafir."

Chapter 2

Taylor and Daphne approached the corral closest to the main building, riding at a jog — which Daphne, using the terms of English-style riding, would have called a trot. Pixie hurried behind, her short legs scurrying to keep up.

Plum Mason and Shafir, a young, untrained Arabian mare, eyed each other in the middle of the corral. Plum held a lunge line that was looped around Shafir's neck. In her hand was a lunge whip. She stood with the line in her left hand and the whip in her right as she tried to make Shafir walk circles around her.

As they drew nearer, Taylor sized up the body

language of both Plum and Shafir. Plum's slim shoulders were tight, slightly hunched with tension. Her pointed chin was raised, almost as though she were trying to stretch herself taller than the chestnut Arabian. Shafir's ears were not quite flat, but they were back, and her tail was swishing, sure signs of the horse's annoyance.

Shafir turned and started to walk away. Plum gripped the line, pulling back, but Shafir was determined to go and dragged Plum along. The girl dug her heels into the dirt, kicking up dust until Shafir stopped. Stepping quickly toward the horse, she whacked the mare's withers hard with the lunge whip.

Shafir's ears flattened against her head as she flinched away from the impact, making Plum lose her balance for a moment.

Daphne reached the corral gate first, quickly dismounted, and hurried inside. "What are you doing?" she asked.

"Excuse me?" Plum replied haughtily.

"What are you doing?" Daphne repeated, this time speaking pointedly, her voice tinged with irritation. "A lunge whip is for guiding a horse, not hitting her!"

Taylor dismounted from Prince Albert. She hitched

him to the corral fence and then did the same to Mandy. There was no need to worry about Pixie wandering off; wherever Prince Albert was, that's where Pixie would be.

As Taylor let herself into the corral, she saw that Plum and Daphne were embroiled in a full-out, heated argument. Taylor's first reaction was relief that Daphne had taken Plum on instead of leaving it to her. Even Plum — queen at the Pheasant Valley Middle School where they were both in the eighth grade — had to be impressed by Daphne, who'd been class president at the middle school before moving on to PV High.

"I leased this horse from the ranch, which means I am entitled to come here whenever I want and do whatever I want with her," Plum insisted.

"No, not whatever you want," Daphne shot back. "You knew when you took the lease that Shafir needs to be trained."

"Well, that's what I'm doing," Plum replied.

A girl with long dark curls who was dressed in jeans and a dark green hoodie strode purposefully out of the main building toward the corral. "What's the trouble here?" fourteen-year-old Mercedes Gonzalez asked in her usual take-charge manner.

11

"You said I could take Shafir, didn't you?" Plum said.

"Yeah. You leased her, right?" Mercedes replied.

"But Shafir isn't ready to ride," Taylor reminded Mercedes.

Mercedes shrugged and then gestured toward Plum. "She holds a lease."

"That entitles her to ride, not to train," Daphne argued.

"I don't know," Mercedes said. "Does it?"

The three girls looked at one another uncertainly. A lease gave Plum the right to ride Shafir whenever she wanted, but could she also train her? That was something Taylor had assumed she, Daphne, and Mercedes would be doing. Taylor had been eager to learn from the two more experienced girls how to bring an untrained horse along.

"No, I don't think it does," Daphne insisted. "Shafir is still the property of Wildwood Stables."

"We'll just talk to the owner — Mrs. What's-her-name, Flowers or whatever," Plum replied forcefully.

Shafir used this interruption as an opportunity to amble toward Prince Albert, Mandy, and Pixie, who stood on the other side of the fence. Shafir neighed, trotting back and forth in front of them, as though inviting them to play. When Shafir came up next to the fence, Prince Albert sniffed her.

In the next moment, Shafir scooped up a bare stick that had fallen from the spreading maple that grew beside the corral. She pranced with the stick in her mouth, bobbing her head up and down, almost as if she were the leader of a parade.

Taylor wondered who had taught her that trick. They really knew very little about Shafir's past, except that she was a purebred Arabian whose owner had not been able to train her and had then dumped her at the fancy Ross River Ranch. Devon Ross, the owner of Ross River, couldn't use the young mare and had donated her to Wildwood Stables.

"What's she doing?" Plum demanded, pointing at Shafir.

"She's playing," Mercedes informed her. "Arabians are known for it."

Giving Shafir to the ranch had been a generous gift. Daphne estimated Shafir was worth at least $20,000, maybe more. It was so generous, in fact, that it had made Taylor curious. She had searched on the Internet and discovered that Mrs. Ross and Mrs. LeFleur had known each other well as young women. But Mrs. LeFleur clearly disliked Mrs. Ross now. The whole thing was mysterious, and Taylor was determined to discover what had happened.

Taylor spied a bridle draped over the corral fence. A chain shank was fitted over the nosepiece and dangled from the bottom. Taylor knew a chain shank was used to pull down the nose of a horse that wasn't obeying orders. "Were you planning to use that on Shafir?" she asked Plum in an accusing tone.

Plum didn't answer. She kept her focus on Daphne and Mercedes as though Taylor wasn't even there.

"Are you using the chain shank on Shafir?" Taylor asked again.

"Does anyone else hear mosquitoes buzzing?" Plum asked.

Taylor's face reddened with anger. But then she remembered her new plan when dealing with Plum. Daphne had suggested it and it made sense: *Just stop treating her like she's got fangs and claws.* It was the only way she'd be able to get close enough to Plum to make sure she was treating Shafir right.

Taylor felt responsible for Shafir. It was Taylor who'd persuaded Plum that Shafir was a great horse for her to lease. She'd acted out of sheer desperation because Plum was about to lease Prince Albert.

Taylor would not let that happen to Prince Albert. It was a matter of life and death.

In the past, at other ranches, horses that Plum had leased had died. Taylor knew of two, for sure, and suspected there might be others. No one was certain if it was Plum's mistreatment that had killed them or if it was just bad luck. In her heart, Taylor felt positive that Plum's careless aftercare, her feeding methods, or her roughness while riding had something to do with the deaths. Seeing how quick she was to hit Shafir just confirmed that belief.

Ignoring Plum's mosquito remark, Taylor forced a smile onto her face. "I was just wondering, Plum, because I've never started a horse and I'm interested in how it's done." Taylor felt as though she was choking out the words. She hoped they didn't sound as false to Plum as they did to her own ears.

A look of startled amazement came onto Daphne's face and was mirrored in Mercedes's expression. Plum glared at Taylor suspiciously.

"Maybe we could all work together to get Shafir trained," Taylor suggested, holding tight to her false pleasantness as she plunged forward. "Daphne and Mercedes were just telling me how much they wanted to work with you. And I really would like to learn."

Daphne suddenly got it. A look of understanding came over her face, though Mercedes continued to appear baffled. But then she, too, seemed to remember what Daphne and Taylor had told her; the three of them would have to watch Plum with Shafir and they'd have to be nice to Plum to do so.

"We could start right now," Mercedes suggested.

Plum's blue eyes shifted warily from side to side as she weighed the situation. She was mean but not dumb — the sudden change in attitude had put her on guard. "I don't need help," she said.

"It wouldn't be *help*," Taylor pressed on. "We'd all be working on it together."

"Yeah, sorry I got so hot with you before," Daphne

stepped in, on board with Taylor's peacemaking plan. "I didn't realize that you knew about breaking in a horse."

"I've started lots of horses," Mercedes added. "You could learn a lot from me."

Taylor shot Mercedes a look; this was not the right approach to take with Plum. "And I'm sure we'll all learn a lot from Plum, too," Taylor put in.

Plum's hands went to her slim hips. "What's with you, Taylor? Didn't you tell me not to talk to you? What's with the big change?"

"Oh, yeah," Taylor recalled sheepishly. "I'm sorry for saying that. I was thinking of school, and how things are between us at school. But you're a part of Wildwood Stables now and everything should be different here." Taylor was surprised to realize that she nearly believed her own words. "Wildwood Stables is special," she added, which she definitely *did* believe.

Plum eyed her surroundings skeptically. For a moment Taylor saw the ranch as it probably looked to Plum, as if seeing through her eyes: an old main building with a sagging roof; some sheds and smaller buildings, also refreshed in the same red; the corral and two paddocks.

"What's special about it?" Plum challenged. "It doesn't seem so great to me."

Then why don't you leave? Taylor thought, but forced herself to stay quiet. She thought of Wildwood Stables as the best place in the world. She was almost glad Plum couldn't see what was so wonderful about it. The feeling was too deep and personal to share with someone Taylor disliked as much she disliked Plum Mason.

"I wouldn't try to put that bridle on Shafir right away," Daphne suggested. "She's never been tacked up before, not even a halter. Why don't you walk her on the lead? If that goes well, then you can stand in the center of the corral and work circles. Try to get her to obey some simple voice commands, too."

"That's what I was going to do," Plum replied.

Then what were the bridle and chain shank for? Taylor wondered, but again stayed silent.

A green compact car drove into the ranch and parked. A woman in her early sixties with thick glasses and a poof of curly brown hair emerged. "Good day, ladies," Mrs. LeFleur said brightly from the other side of the corral fence. "It's so lovely to see all of you working together. How is Shafir coming along?"

18

"Plum is going to start her on voice commands," Taylor volunteered brightly.

"Wonderful," said Mrs. LeFleur, smiling. "Taylor, Mercedes, and Daphne, when you're available, please come to see me in the office. I have something important I must speak to you about."

Chapter 3

"All right, ladies, here's the thing," said Mrs. LeFleur, leaning against the old, scratched desk in her office at the front of the main building. She looked at Taylor, Mercedes, and Daphne, all sitting on the ripped leather couch. "As of next week, I am flat out of money."

"How can that be?" Mercedes questioned. "We have Dana signed up for therapeutic riding and Plum's lease on Shafir."

"The first month's payment on the lease went to the big order of hay that's coming today from Westheimer's Ranch. Ralph Westheimer and I shared the expense of buying a bulk order and it was a good deal."

"If it was such a good deal why did it cost so much?" Mercedes asked.

"Because we bought so much of it," Mrs. LeFleur replied.

"At least the horses will eat well," Taylor said, hoping to add a positive note.

"They'll eat great, but where will they live if I can't keep up the ranch?" Mrs. LeFleur countered.

"Doesn't the money from letting Dana use Prince Albert for her therapy lessons help?" Taylor asked.

"Dana's mother paid me for a month's worth of lessons, and I'll use that to pay the farrier, who's coming today to shoe the horses. Prince Albert and Pixie need it desperately. Their hooves have completely overgrown their shoes. If there's any of that money left, I'll bring in a vet to check out the horses. I can't put that off much longer."

"We have that ad saying we take in boards running this week in the *Pennysaver*," Mercedes reminded Mrs. LeFleur.

"Yes, and it already brought in some calls. I'm meeting with two people who might want to board their horses here. Any other ideas on how we might drum up some business?"

"My dad told me there used to be rodeos here," Taylor recalled.

"Your father came here as a child?" Mrs. LeFleur asked.

"My social studies teacher did, too," Taylor replied. It had actually been Mr. Romano who'd first told her about the old ranch.

"What's his name?"

"Mr. Romano."

"John Romano?"

"I don't know. Maybe. Yes, I think his name might be John," Taylor replied. "Do you know him?"

"Possibly, long ago," Mrs. LeFleur said, a wistful note entering her voice.

Taylor realized that she had no idea where Mrs. LeFleur's home was. "Do you live in Pheasant Valley, Mrs. LeFleur?"

"Not anymore. I live in Bronxville."

"Near the city?" Mercedes asked.

"Yes."

"But you lived here once?" Taylor pressed. "You went to *this* ranch?"

"At one time. Yes," Mrs. LeFleur said with a nod. "Is your father little Stevie Henry, by any chance?"

That made Taylor chuckle. "He's not so little anymore."

"No. I guess not."

This revelation that Mrs. LeFleur had known her father when he was a boy fascinated Taylor. She couldn't wait to talk to him about it. Maybe he knew the story of Mrs. LeFleur's past. And if he didn't, perhaps Mr. Romano did.

"A rodeo, huh?" Mrs. LeFleur said, rubbing her hands together thoughtfully. "I do recall that, yes. It might be a great way to get people to come down to see the ranch. Have you ever ridden in a rodeo, Taylor?"

Taylor missed Mrs. LeFleur's question. She was focused out the front window, looking to the corral where Plum had Shafir on a long lunge line jogging in a circle. Unbidden, the Arabian abruptly turned toward the center, heading toward Plum.

Instinctively, Taylor stood up, ready to run out to the corral at the first sign that Plum was going to discipline

Shafir roughly. Noticing what Taylor was seeing, Mercedes and Daphne rose from the couch, too. Mrs. LeFleur also turned toward the window.

They watched as Plum panicked and dropped her end of the line, running from the advancing horse.

Shafir chased Plum around the corral at a jogging pace, while Plum screamed for help.

"Shafir thinks it's a game," Taylor realized, laughing.

Daphne and Mercedes fell onto each other, chuckling gleefully.

Mrs. LeFleur seemed about to join in, but her smile quickly faded. "She could fall right in Shafir's path and get hurt. Daphne, go help her, please," Mrs. LeFleur requested.

Daphne left the office, and through the window they saw her approach the corral at a half run. Taylor bit down on her smile as Plum jumped behind Daphne, hiding from Shafir.

Daphne took a horse treat from the pocket of her sweatshirt, unwrapped it, and offered the treat to Shafir. The frisky Arabian gobbled it from Daphne's palm. It was all that was needed to distract her from the fun of chasing Plum.

Mrs. LeFleur turned to Taylor, smiling a little. "You enjoyed that, no doubt?"

Taylor could no longer suppress her grin. "No, not at all," she joked. "That was terrible. Poor Plum!"

Mrs. LeFleur's gaze lingered at the window a moment more before she turned away. "Back to business — what were we saying about rodeos?"

"Just that they were held here once and maybe would be a good way to get customers now," Taylor said as she and Mercedes resumed their seats on the couch.

"I don't think any of us could ride in a rodeo," Mercedes said. "They're kind of rough. But I saw a games event once. It wasn't as intense as an actual rodeo with bull riding and roping. I'm trying to remember what kinds of games they did."

"Do you mean events like barrel racing, and stalls, poles, and ride a buck?" Mrs. LeFleur asked.

"What are those?" Taylor questioned.

"Different horse games," Mrs. LeFleur answered.

"We don't have enough horses for all that," Mercedes pointed out.

"But what if we invited people to participate and they

could bring their horses here? It might result in some new boarders," Mrs. LeFleur replied.

A tall, blond young man in overalls appeared at the office door. "Hi, Rick," Taylor greeted him. She knew Ralph Westheimer's ranch hand from when she had taken riding lessons over at the rustic Westheimer's Ranch. Rick had also helped with the rescue of Prince Albert and Pixie.

"Hey, Taylor," he replied. "I see you got the two rescues out there. They look a whole lot better now."

"Do you really think so?" Taylor asked, pleased by his words.

"Yeah, I can't see the ribs on the big black quarter anymore, and you got the little pony cleaned up nice."

"Thanks," Taylor said.

"They're being reshoed today," Mrs. LeFleur added.

"Great," Rick said. "You've done a good job with them. I don't know how you pulled it off."

"A lot of luck and a fairy godmother," Taylor replied, smiling at Mrs. LeFleur.

"Coupled with her ingenuity and grit," Mrs. LeFleur said, smiling back.

"Grit?" Taylor asked.

"Your stubborn toughness," Mrs. LeFleur explained.

"Is that good?" Taylor inquired uncertainly.

"*I* think so," Mrs. LeFleur said, nodding.

"Mrs. LeFleur, the hay you bought with Ralph is on my truck. Where do you want it?" Rick asked.

"Around back in the feed house, near the outside stalls. Mercedes, would you show Rick where I mean?"

"Okay," Mercedes said, getting off the couch.

"Rick, do you know anything about horse games or gaming events?" Taylor asked quickly before they could leave.

"Sure. What do you want to know?"

"We're thinking of running an event like that here," Mrs. LeFleur said.

Daphne returned to the office. "Plum has Shafir going in a circle again," she reported. "She'll be okay."

"Come on, Rick. I'll show you to the feed house where we keep the hay," Mercedes said, passing Daphne in the doorway.

"I can come back to tell you about the game events after we do this," Rick said to Mrs. LeFleur, stepping away from the door. "There's a lot about it online, too."

                              *   *   *

Mrs. LeFleur received a call from one of her potential horse boarders, which ended the business meeting for the time being. Taylor and Daphne left the office and strolled together back outside.

"I don't believe this," Daphne suddenly cried.

Shafir was alone in the corral. Mandy, Prince Albert, and Pixie were still on the outside of the corral watching the Arabian, who was once more bobbing her head with her stick between her lips, dragging the lead line behind her.

The back of Plum's mom's black SUV was turning the corner onto Wildwood Lane.

"Plum just left Shafir, still attached to the lead line!" Taylor cried.

"That girl is too much!" Daphne remarked as they hurried into the corral.

"Tell me about it!" Taylor said. "I guess she thinks we're her servants."

"I guess so," Daphne said, approaching Shafir from the front. "Whoa, girl," she commanded. "Whoa."

Shafir did a small two-step dance and then turned away as if she didn't understand what was being asked of her. "You know what whoa means," Daphne insisted. "You obeyed that command for me earlier today." She approached Shafir, looking at her directly.

Shafir took four steps away but then stopped and allowed Daphne to pick up the end of the lunge line that was dragging in the dirt. "Good girl," Daphne praised.

Taylor watched as Daphne calmed Shafir and then led her back toward the stable, admiring Daphne's natural ease with horses. Daphne knew how to let Shafir keep her dignity while still insisting that the horse obey commands.

Mercedes came around from the back of the main building with Rick. With them was a guy who appeared to be about fourteen or fifteen. He had dark brown hair and looked slim yet broad-shouldered in his jeans, plaid shirt, and cowboy boots.

Taylor had never seen him, which she found odd. Pheasant Valley was big but not that heavily populated. She recognized most kids around her age because she'd seen them at school.

And she would definitely have noticed this guy.

"Here's the horse we were telling you about," Mercedes was saying as she guided him over to Prince Albert. "Taylor owns him now, and she owns Pixie, too, of course."

"Hi, I'm Eric," the boy said, raising his hand in greeting. "Mercedes and Rick were just telling me about how you helped rescue these guys and all. Cool."

Prince Albert sputtered as Taylor petted his side. "Yeah, Pixie and Prince Albert love each other a lot, so it's good we've been able to keep them together," Taylor said, noticing that Eric's eyes were hazel green.

"Eric knows a lot about Western games, it turns out. And he's willing to work with us," Mercedes said.

"Awesome!" Taylor cried, letting her smile get wider than she meant to. "But . . . I mean . . . why are you willing to do that?"

"I don't know," Eric admitted with a shrug, "for the fun of it, maybe. I was a junior counselor at a Western riding camp last summer and we did a lot of that kind of thing. I just miss it, I guess."

"Eric works with us at the ranch after school now," Rick explained.

"Where do you go to school?" Taylor asked.

"The Johnson School in Dobbs Ferry."

Expensive, was Taylor's first thought.

"I get a lot of scholarship help," Eric added as though he'd read Taylor's mind.

Taylor was impressed. A scholarship to the Johnson School meant that Eric was smart.

"We'd better get back to the ranch," Rick said, heading toward his flatbed truck.

"Later," Eric said, waving to the girls as he followed Rick.

Taylor returned his wave. "Bye!" She watched him climb in behind Rick and kept her eyes on the truck as it stirred up a small cloud of dust on its way out of the ranch.

"Don't your cheeks hurt?" Mercedes asked Taylor.

Taylor's hands flew up to both sides of her face. "No. Why should they?"

"Because you're standing there grinning like a crazy girl," Mercedes said.

Chapter 4

*L*ater that afternoon, Taylor stood beside Prince Albert in the central aisle that separated the inside stalls of the main building. She had unsaddled him, leaving only his halter on, and was running a body brush over his coat when a man in his midthirties with longish black hair and a salt-and-pepper beard approached her. "I'm Norman, the farrier," he introduced himself as he tied on a full leather apron over his protruding belly. "Is this guy Prince Albert?"

"Yes, he is."

Norman gave Prince Albert's flank a friendly pat. "Hey, big fella."

Prince Albert swung his head around to see what was happening. He sputtered and nodded.

Taylor smiled at her horse's response. Lately she had noticed that when spoken to, Prince Albert always replied in some way, as if he were actually communicating. Maybe it was only the sound of a human voice that made him react, but it was fun to think he was really answering.

Crouching, Norman got slightly in front of Prince Albert's left hind foot and lifted it. He emitted a low whistle. "Boy, is this shoe overgrown. It's not dirty, though."

"I just cleaned his hoof out with a pick," Taylor said.

"Good job," Norman commended her. "I guess I'll get started on him."

"He has a therapeutic riding lesson in ten minutes," Taylor told him. "Could you work with Shafir first?" She pointed to the Arabian who had been returned to her stall.

Mrs. LeFleur joined them. "Norman, maybe Daphne or Mercedes should help you with Shafir," she suggested. "Shafir is very high-spirited."

"Of course she is, she's an Arabian," Norman said as he set Prince Albert's hoof down. "I can handle her."

While Mrs. LeFleur introduced Norman to Shafir, Taylor clipped a lead line to Prince Albert's halter. Opening Pixie's stall so the pony could follow Prince Albert, Taylor led both of them outside.

Taylor halted Prince Albert and Pixie so she could open the corral gate. Lois, the therapeutic riding instructor, was just getting out of her car. She was an attractive dark-skinned woman in her late twenties. Lois had her degree in psychology but was still finishing her certification as a horse therapist at the nearby state university. "Hi, there," she called to Taylor.

Another car pulled in. The driver was a heavy blonde woman named Alice. With her was Dana, her petite seven-year-old daughter who had been diagnosed as having autism. Even though Dana had never ridden a horse before, the pale blonde girl had instantly fallen in love with Prince Albert and refused to work with any other horse.

As soon as Dana got out of the car, she saw Prince Albert and her eyes lit up with happiness. Quivering slightly from head to toe, she lifted her hands and stretched her fingers, fluttering her palms with excited joy.

Lois placed her hand lightly on Dana's shoulder and gently guided her toward the horse. "Come see your friend, Dana," she coached.

Dana reached up to pet Prince Albert's muzzle. "Did you bring him anything?" Lois asked.

Nodding excitedly, Dana dug in her jeans pocket and withdrew an apple. A look of unease swept her delicate face. "Don't be afraid," Taylor encouraged her. "Make your hand flat and hold the apple up to him."

Dana glanced up at Prince Albert uncertainly.

"You can do it," Lois added.

Dana balanced the apple on her flattened palm, lifting it to Prince Albert.

Chomp! Half the apple disappeared into Prince Albert's mouth while the other half tumbled to the ground. Dana jumped away, laughing. "Ew!" she shouted, smiling, as she wiped Prince Albert's slobber onto her jeans. "Ew!"

"Give him the other half," Taylor suggested.

Dana shook her head. "It's dirty now."

Taylor lifted the apple and cleaned it on her sweatshirt. "He won't mind," she said, handing it back to Dana.

Once again the girl offered the apple. Prince Albert

gobbled it and then his long tongue licked every inch of Dana's fingers, searching for any last traces of apple goodness that might remain. This sent Dana into a fit of giggles. "He likes me!" she sang out. Although her nose was wrinkled, she allowed the licking, keeping her hand to Prince Albert's mouth. "He likes me!" she said again.

"He likes you a lot," Taylor confirmed. "Scratch his nose. He loves when you do that." Dana reached for Prince Albert's nose and ran her short nails lightly up and down his muzzle.

Prince Albert whinnied his appreciation, which made Dana laugh.

"He says thanks. He can't reach that spot on his own," Taylor told her.

"It's great to see her so happy," Alice remarked, her eyes glistening fondly at her daughter. "Lois, how soon do you think it will be before you have her riding?"

"I think she could be mounted and walking by next week," Lois replied.

"Next week!" Taylor cried before she could stop herself. "I mean, isn't that kind of fast?"

"I really want to get Dana in the saddle as soon as possible," Lois replied. "The even pacing of a steady gait and the balance work can be very positive for children with autism."

Prince Albert had to be willing to let Dana ride him by next week. If he wasn't — and Dana had to switch to another horse — Prince Albert would no longer be of any value to the ranch at all.

Taylor lay on her bed with her socked feet on the wall and her head hanging over the side. She'd just washed her long brown hair and it hung dripping into a bath towel she'd dropped on the floor. Her cell phone was pressed to the side of her face as she spoke to her best friend, Travis Ryan. "Prince Albert was so good with Dana today," she told him. "He's so patient and sweet with her. I filmed the whole lesson with Lois's video camera like I did last time. And guess what? We're going to have a horse games event at Wildwood."

"Cool beans," Travis said. "What kind of games?"

The first thing Taylor had done when she got home from the ranch was to do an Internet search of games played on horseback. There were lots of them, she discovered. "There's one called stalls, which is like musical chairs," she told Travis. "A kind of grid is laid out as if they're stalls, and there's one less stall space than there are riders. When the ref, or whoever, blows a whistle, all the riders have to ride into a stall, and the one who doesn't get a stall loses. Each time, they take away one of the stall spaces until there's only one rider and horse left and they're the winners."

"How are you going to learn to do all that stuff?" Travis asked.

Instantly, an image of Eric's hazel green eyes popped into Taylor's mind.

"Some guy over at Westheimer's is going to work with us," she said, deliberately keeping her voice nonchalant, as though what she was telling him was unimportant. Taylor wasn't sure why she was making this extra effort to seem disinterested. Travis was her best and oldest friend; they'd been friends since third grade — but he wasn't her boyfriend. It had never been anything like that. Still, she felt awkward about discussing Eric with Travis.

"Why would a guy from Westheimer's work with Wildwood?" Travis questioned.

"He says it's fun."

"It does sound fun," Travis agreed.

"Why don't you take a lesson on Mandy?" Taylor suggested. Travis didn't ride, but Taylor was dying to get him started.

"No money," he replied. "There was a great online auction on Spider-Man graphic novels. Mom let me use her PayPal and now I have to pay her back. I used all my birthday money, but it was worth it." Travis's greatest thrill in life was to get a new or rare superhero graphic novel or comic.

"You don't have to take a lesson with Daphne right away. I could get you started, and, of course, you don't have to pay me."

"Naw. I'm not the horseback-riding type," Travis declined.

"You're just chicken," Taylor challenged him.

"Am not!"

"Then get on a horse," Taylor insisted. As she spoke, Taylor was suddenly looking at her mother's sneaker-clad feet.

"This room is a mess, Taylor," said Jennifer Henry, pushing her blonde curls from her face. "And now you have a soaking wet towel on the floor."

"I have to go," Taylor said, pulling herself onto her bed.

"Parental unit in need of attention?" Travis guessed.

"Yep. Talk to you later."

"Okay, later."

"It smells like a stable in here, Taylor. Your dirty clothes reek of horses," Jennifer chided.

"Sorry."

Jennifer began picking up the dirty clothes strewn across the floor and tossing them into Taylor's neon green pop-up hamper. "You have to keep this room neater," she said. "Now that I'm so busy with the business you have to help me out more."

Taylor's parents had divorced at the beginning of the previous spring. Even though Taylor assumed her father must pay her mother some money to help with Taylor's expenses, their household money seemed to have dried up after her father left. There were no more dessert treats in the fridge or weekend movies, and her eighth-grade back-to-school shopping had consisted of a new pair of sneakers.

A tight budget was the reason Taylor had stopped

taking riding lessons over at Westheimer's Ranch. But now her mom's new catering business was starting to do well, thanks in large part to the great word of mouth from a luncheon Jennifer had catered over at the swanky Ross River Ranch.

"Mom?" Taylor asked as she bent to pick up more dirty laundry. "Did you ever go down to Wildwood Stables when you were a kid?"

"No. I didn't ride. Your dad did, though. I thought he told you that."

"He did. It's just that Mrs. LeFleur thought she knew Dad, and Mr. Romano, too."

"I don't know. Ask him about it."

"Did you ever see Mrs. LeFleur around town when you were a kid?"

Sitting on Taylor's bed, Jennifer tilted her head thoughtfully. "I don't think I've ever met her before. You could call Grandma and ask. Why is it so important?"

"I did an Internet search and found an old photo of Mrs. Ross and Mrs. LeFleur. Mrs. LeFleur was in Mrs. Ross's wedding party. It said she was the matron of honor. Why didn't they say maid of honor?"

"She must have been married already when she was in the wedding party. If the woman is married they say matron instead of maid. But what's this about?"

"You know how Mrs. LeFleur dislikes Mrs. Ross so much? And Mrs. Ross just up and gave Shafir to her. I was just wondering what happened between them."

"Hmmm, now you have *me* curious," Jennifer admitted as she stood up and lifted the now full hamper. "Straighten the shoes you've tossed in that corner," she instructed.

Taylor got to work sorting out the sneakers, flip-flops, and bedroom slippers. Her new brown cowboy boots with the embossed western designs stood on their own, already cleaned with spray-on leather cleaner and buffed to a shine. "Mom, we're going to have a games event sometime soon," Taylor said, and went on to tell Jennifer about the different types of games. "This guy Eric, who works at Westheimer's Ranch, is going to come over and show us how to play."

"That sounds great," Jennifer said as she carried the hamper to the bedroom door. "Hopefully, it will bring in a lot of business."

Taylor nodded and went back to sorting her shoes. As she worked, she thought about what it would be like to learn the games from Eric. "Mom," she said, catching Jennifer just as she was about to leave, "when was the first time you liked a boy?"

"You don't mean in the way that you and Travis like each other," Jennifer clarified.

"No," Taylor said, rolling her eyes. "You know what I mean. When did you first *like* like a boy?"

Jennifer's eyes drifted to the ceiling as though she were trying to see back to a memory buried deep in her past. "I liked Andy Kelly in the eighth grade," she recalled. "I thought about him day and night."

"Was he nice?"

"I don't know. He never spoke to me. Why do you ask? Is there someone special you like?"

"No," Taylor said, turning her attention back to her shoes. "I was just wondering."

Chapter 5

On Monday, Taylor walked into Pheasant Valley Middle School with Travis. "Does my hair look okay?" Travis asked Taylor, rubbing the flat, bristly top of his white-blond crew cut self-consciously. The stocky boy's wide, pleasant face looked particularly moonlike since he'd just cropped his hair even shorter than usual over the weekend.

"It looks good," Taylor assured him.

They turned a hallway corner on the way to their lockers and nearly crashed into Plum and the crowd of girls she always traveled with. "Watch it," one of them sneered.

"*You* watch it," Travis shot back.

"Sorry," Taylor apologized. "How was the rest of your training session with Shafir?" she asked Plum pleasantly. Even though she desperately wanted to give Plum an earful about just leaving Shafir with a lead line dragging behind, Taylor forced herself not to.

"Great," Plum replied in a flat voice. "Fine. Whatever." Plum angled away from Taylor, signaling that their conversation was over.

Taylor pretended she didn't notice the snub and stepped to the side so she was back in Plum's sight line. "Shafir's a great horse, and you're doing a terrific job with her."

Plum's head snapped around. "I said, yeah, whatever — can you drop it?" Hands on hips, eyebrows raised disdainfully, all of Plum's friends stared at Taylor with annoyance.

"Okay. See you later," Taylor said, walking away quickly with Travis by her side. When they were far enough away, she fanned herself to cool down the burning blush of embarrassment she knew was flaming on her cheeks.

"Before you think I'm crazy, there's a good

explanation," Taylor said to Travis as her fingers flapped in front of her red face.

"Yeah, I know what it is already."

"You do? What?" she questioned.

"It's obvious I'm still in bed dreaming," he said, not smiling. "There is no way what I just saw really happened. It was too weird."

"I know it was," Taylor agreed. She explained to him how she felt responsible for Shafir being leased by Plum and that she had to stay close to Plum to ensure the horse's safety.

"Oh, yeah, Plum the horse killer," Travis murmured, recalling what Taylor had told him about the two equine deaths Plum was suspected of having caused.

Just then, Mr. Romano came walking toward them. "Everything okay?"

"Everything's fine," Travis answered. "I'm just having a strange dream and you're all in it."

Mr. Romano stopped short. "What?"

"Don't listen to him. He's crazy," Taylor said.

Travis pressed his hand on his chest in an expression of shock and dismay. "*I'm* crazy? I don't think *you* should talk about anyone being crazy."

Taylor overlooked Travis's comment as the two of them fell into step with Mr. Romano and moved down the hall with him. "Mr. Romano, when you used to go to Wildwood Stables as a boy, was there someone named Bernice LeFleur who worked there or rode there?"

"Wait a minute," he said, slowing his pace. "I do know that name. I remember her very well — Jimmy LeFleur's mother."

"Did he ride with you down at the ranch?" Taylor asked.

Mr. Romano nodded. "He was a good rider, too. And Mrs. LeFleur was an instructor there. I saw her jump once at a show they gave. She was amazing. Her uncle owned the place, I'm pretty sure."

"Mrs. LeFleur inherited the ranch — so the woman you're remembering is definitely her," Taylor said. "When was the last time you saw them?"

Mr. Romano stopped and a serious expression came over him. "I can tell you the exact day," he said. "I was there the afternoon Jimmy LeFleur got thrown from his horse and had to be taken away in an ambulance. I never saw Jimmy or his mother again after that."

* * *

Mrs. LeFleur and her son were on Taylor's mind as she rode her bike on Wildwood Lane and turned into the ranch at the new sign. In black swirling writing against a sky blue background, the sign announced:

WILDWOOD STABLES
HOME OF HAPPY HORSES AND PONIES
ALL EQUINE LOVERS WELCOME
Horses Boarded * Riding Lessons * Trail Rides Available

The sign made Taylor smile every time she passed it. She was always tempted to take a marker and add *The best place in the world!!!* at the bottom, but she didn't have the nerve. It was the way she thought of Wildwood Stables, though — as a magical place full of happy energy.

Taylor's smile faded as she continued pedaling past the sign and into the ranch. Mr. Romano's story about Jimmy LeFleur didn't go with Taylor's idea of only good things happening at Wildwood. What had happened to Jimmy? Why hadn't he and Mrs. LeFleur ever come back after that day?

Leaning her bike against the big maple with the knobby roots, she looked into the corral. Daphne was leading a little girl of about five on Pixie's saddled back. Two of the girl's friends stood off to the side with a woman, waiting their turn. Nearby in the corral, Prince Albert grazed along the fence posts, casually watching the ranch's first pony ride.

Prince Albert noticed Taylor's arrival and walked over to greet her, sticking his head over the fence. Taylor kissed his nose, rubbing his soft muzzle. From her sweatshirt pocket, she took out one of the baby carrots she'd sneaked from the raw vegetable platter her mother would be serving at a party she was catering that evening. Prince Albert instantly grabbed it in his teeth.

"Don't act like you're starving," Taylor teased him as she presented him a second carrot. "You're getting fed."

"He's a nice-looking horse."

Taylor jumped, startled as she turned to face Eric. "Wow! You scared me. I didn't realize you were there."

"Sorry. I didn't mean to creep up on you," Eric apologized.

Taylor's lips were suddenly parched and her mind had gone blank. Even though Eric was looking at her expectantly, assuming she was about to reply, she some-how couldn't speak.

Prince Albert whinnied and stomped the ground. "I guess I startled him, too," Eric said.

Letting out a shrill neigh, Prince Albert turned and kicked the fence with his back legs.

"Stand back," Taylor told Eric. The boy took a few large steps backward.

Prince Albert kicked the fence again. "Albert, stop that!" Taylor commanded. "It's okay. He's not going to hurt us. Calm down, boy."

"I didn't mean to upset him. What did I do?" Eric asked.

"It's not you. He doesn't like guys. Good thing you're not wearing a baseball cap. He hates those."

Eric walked toward the main building, checking over his shoulder as he went.

Prince Albert turned back around so he was facing the fence again. With ears still flattened, he bared his teeth in Eric's direction and neighed fiercely once more.

"Is something wrong?" Daphne called over to Taylor.

"It's just the guy problem," Taylor shouted back.

Daphne looked to Eric standing by the main building

and nodded her understanding. "I almost forgot about that," she said, returning to her third pony ride.

Taylor stepped onto the bottom rung of the split-rail fence and petted Prince Albert's forelock. With the other hand she took out another carrot.

At the sight of the carrot, Prince Albert's ears perked up straight again, and his rapidly swishing tail slowed and then stopped.

"It's all right," Taylor soothed him. "You don't have to be scared of him."

Prince Albert snorted, as though blowing off the last of his aggressive anger, and then snapped the carrot from Taylor's palm.

It made Taylor furious every time she remembered that some man, probably one wearing a baseball cap, had mistreated Prince Albert so harshly that now the gentle horse feared all men. It was the only explanation she could think of for Prince Albert's reaction.

With a final fond stroke to Prince Albert's head, Taylor hopped off the fence and approached Eric. "Sorry about that. Albert hates all guys."

Eric looked over to Albert. "Hey, you! I resent that!" he called, although Taylor could tell he was joking.

"It's nothing personal," Taylor assured him. "Someone must have been harsh with him."

"All horses have their little personality quirks. They're not so different from people," Eric said easily. "Maybe I can get him to like me."

"Good luck on that one," Taylor said skeptically, though she thought that if anyone could do it, it would be Eric.

"Are you ready to try some horse games today?" Eric asked. "Daphne said that as soon as she's done with the pony rides, we can start."

"Great. What horse will you ride?"

"Rick agreed to trailer my horse here."

"What kind is she?"

"Jojo's a he, a Tennessee walking horse gelding. I had to work for two summers to buy him. And I was only able to afford it because I got a good price for him from a guy who was moving and couldn't keep him anymore."

"Why don't you board him here?" Taylor suggested.

"I work after school part-time for Ralph. I'd feel weird boarding Jojo somewhere else," Eric explained. "Do you know if Prince Albert has ever played horse games before?"

"Daphne taught him to play halters recently."

"I don't know that one," Eric said.

"It's also called bandanna snatch," Taylor recalled.

"Oh, bandanna snatch. Yeah, that's a fun game. Does he know any others?"

"I guess we'll find out," Taylor said. "He obeys voice commands really well, so somebody trained him. But I don't know too much else about him."

"Why don't you call the American Quarter Horse Association?" Eric suggested.

"Mrs. LeFleur did, and they told us the name of his parents and who owned them. All we really know about him is that he's pure quarter horse and he was born up in Saratoga Springs."

"There's a racetrack up there," Eric said.

"Really? Do you think he might have been a race-horse?"

"Maybe. A quarter horse runs very fast for a —"

"— quarter of a mile," Taylor finished. "Ralph told me that, too."

"You know Ralph?"

"He taught me to ride."

"Me, too!" Eric said, laughing at the coincidence. "He doesn't say much." Eric folded his arms and tilted his head, imitating Ralph Westheimer. "Back straight. Heels down."

"That's right! That's just how he is." Taylor also folded her arms in imitation of Ralph. "Chin up! Shoulders back!"

"He must say that stuff in his sleep," Eric added, chuckling.

Eric's really nice, Taylor decided, every bit as nice as she'd somehow known he would be.

Chapter 6

Taylor was leading Pixie and Prince Albert but halted them outside the big paddock closest to the pasture. She ran to open the paddock gate and held it for Daphne to ride through on Mandy. Behind Daphne, Eric rode in on Jojo. His bay Tennessee walking horse had a large head with a straight profile. The gelding's high-set tail was similar to Shafir's high tail, though not as brushlike.

Mercedes and Travis were already inside the paddock, waiting for them. "Look what I found in the storage building over there," Mercedes said. Behind her were three large barrels standing on end.

Taylor led Pixie and Prince Albert to the gate but

stopped there. She was nervous about how Prince Albert would react to Travis and Eric.

"Yeah, you found them, but who dragged them out of the building?" Travis said grumpily.

"We both did," Mercedes insisted, folding her arms.

Travis's jaw dropped. "Are you kidding me? You pulled them from the gate to here after I lugged them all the way over?"

"Oh, wah-wah, stop crying," Mercedes dismissed him.

"Thanks, Travis," Taylor said to smooth things over. "They must have had barrel races here back in the day."

"Is someone going to ride the pony?" Eric asked.

"No, but Pixie likes to be where Prince Albert is," Taylor explained.

Dismounting, Eric rolled the barrels on their sides until an invisible line between them would have formed a triangle. Using his feet as a measure, he walked between the barrels, adjusting their distance from each other. "There's got to be ninety feet between barrels one and two; one hundred and five feet between barrels one and three and between two and three," Eric explained.

"What do you do with them?" Travis wanted to know.

"The idea is to ride around in a three-leaf clover pattern," Eric explained, drawing in the dirt with a stick.

"That doesn't sound too hard," Taylor remarked from the gate. She hoped that by standing there she was giving Prince Albert time to see that Eric and Travis weren't menacing or mean.

"The person who rides around all three barrels fastest wins," Mercedes said.

"That's what makes it tough," Daphne added. "To pick up time, you have to get as close to the barrels as you can without knocking them over."

"For now, just try out the course and see how you do," Eric suggested.

"This is usually a girls' event," Mercedes said.

"What do you mean?" Taylor asked.

"It started out as the Girls' Rodeo," Mercedes explained. "I read a book about it. The Girls' Rodeo is called the WPRA now, the Women's Professional Rodeo Association."

"How did you learn to barrel race, Eric?" Daphne asked.

"I was a junior counselor at a western riding camp last summer." He nodded toward Jojo. "It helped me earn the money to buy him."

"Yeah? You can't afford a horse on a counselor's pay," Mercedes challenged.

"No, but I had other money saved," Eric replied.

"And he got a good price on Jojo," Taylor added.

Taylor hoped that enough time had passed for Prince Albert to get used to the two boys, so she took hold of his bridle and began to lead him into the paddock. At once, Prince Albert whipped his head back and forth, breaking Taylor's hold on him. His two front feet lifted from the ground as he stomped down hard on the dirt, sputtering. Then he veered to the side and ran in a circle.

"Albert! Stop!" Taylor commanded.

"Don't let him do that!" Mercedes said, running toward them.

Casting a look of exasperation at Taylor, Mercedes hurried to Prince Albert, who was about to begin a second circle, and grabbed his bridle strap. "You stop that! Bad boy!"

To Taylor's surprise, he settled down to a walk.

"Get me that lead line on the fence," Mercedes commanded. Taylor brought it to her, and Mercedes clipped the line onto Prince Albert's halter. "You are on time-out," Mercedes told Prince Albert as she led him toward the main building, with Pixie trotting behind.

Taylor propped her elbow on the half door to Prince Albert's stable and rested her chin on her hand. Prince Albert sputtered, and Taylor could tell he wasn't happy to be back in his stall. Mercedes had offered Pixie the chance to stay outside in the corral, but she couldn't be made to leave Prince Albert's side and so she, too, was now in her stall beside the black horse.

Feeling bad for her horse, Taylor reached into her pocket for the last of her carrots.

"Don't give him a treat," Mercedes scolded from inside Shafir's stall across the aisle as she looped a lead line around the Arabian's head. "He's being punished."

"It's not his fault that he's scared of boys and men," Taylor argued.

"He can't be allowed to break away from you like that," Mercedes insisted. "He's a well-trained horse, and I'm sure he knows better. But you're soft with him, and he knows that, too. He's testing you, like little kids do."

What Mercedes was saying made sense to Taylor, and she put the carrot back in her pocket. "Are you going to work with Shafir?" Taylor asked.

"I want her to watch the barrel-racing work," Mercedes explained. "If she sees Daphne riding Mandy and Eric on Jojo, maybe she'll get the idea of what she's supposed to do."

Shafir's pointy ears were forward, and her head was tilted attentively, almost as though she were following the conversation between Taylor and Mercedes. "I wonder . . . ," Taylor murmured as she pushed herself away from the stall door.

Hurrying down the center aisle, she turned left into the tack room near the front door. Scanning the horse tack quickly, she took a rope halter from a peg and quickly returned to Mercedes and Shafir with it.

"You think you can halter her?" Mercedes asked in a doubtful tone.

"Something tells me she's ready," Taylor replied quietly as she stood in front of Shafir and took out her last baby carrot. "She wants to be involved in the games."

Smelling the treat from across the aisle, Prince Albert whinnied imploringly.

Ignoring him, Taylor offered Shafir the carrot. The Arabian bent her head forward with interest and then grabbed it between her teeth.

"That's a nice girl," Taylor said, stroking her muzzle. She kept talking soothingly and petting Shafir, all the while working the rope harness over her mouth, up her muzzle, and then over her ears. As Taylor had suspected, the mare appeared to be ready for this step.

"Wow! How did you know?" Mercedes asked, impressed.

"I wasn't sure," Taylor admitted. "I only saw that Shafir is interested in everything going on around her, so I thought she might be ready to join in."

Mercedes removed the lead line she'd put over Shafir's neck and took out the loop; then she clipped it to the rope halter. "Come on, Taylor. Let's show her the barrel racing," Mercedes suggested, leading Shafir out of the stall.

"Okay," Taylor replied, stepping into the aisle.

Prince Albert neighed at her. "I know you want a carrot, but I don't have any more," Taylor told him, presenting her empty hands as proof.

Prince Albert just stared expectantly.

"Sorry, fella. I have nothing left," Taylor apologized.

"Taylor, come on!" Mercedes shouted.

"I'm coming," Taylor called back.

When she was halfway up the aisle, Taylor checked over her shoulder. Prince Albert was staring at her. Taylor felt guilty, but she knew she couldn't give in. "I'll get you another carrot later," she muttered guiltily as she ran to catch up with Mercedes.

Chapter 7

Taylor and Travis stood side by side, balancing on the bottom rung of the fence, watching the action inside the paddock. "She's really good," Taylor commented as Daphne sped around the barrels while Eric timed her. Travis nodded, waving away the dust cloud that Mandy's pounding hooves had stirred up.

Taylor looked at Eric standing beside the barrels with his stopwatch and wondered if Eric admired Daphne's skill on horseback. How could he not?

Mercedes stood in the corral off to the side, next to Shafir, both of them watching intently. She had unclipped the Arabian mare from the lead and was furling the line into a loop as she focused on Daphne careening around each barrel at top speed.

"Great, even better than last time," Eric said when Daphne slowed to a walk. "See if you can come even closer to that first barrel next time so you get off to a strong start." He turned to Taylor. "Want to try?"

"You can ride Mandy, if you want," Daphne offered as she swung out of the saddle.

A small knot of nerves formed in Taylor's belly, but she didn't want to give in to it. She wanted Eric to see that Daphne wasn't the only one who could excel at barrel racing. "Okay!" she agreed.

"Good luck," Travis said as Taylor went around to the corral gate. She replied with an anxious thumbs-up.

"Hey, Mercedes told us it was you who harnessed Shafir," Daphne said when Taylor was in the corral. "Nice job! Did she resist you?"

"Not at all," Taylor reported, taking the reins from Daphne.

Taylor stole a sideways glance at Eric, checking to see if he was paying attention to the conversation. She hoped he was impressed that she'd been able to get a halter on the half-wild Arabian.

"Take it slow the first time," Eric advised while Taylor adjusted the stirrups to the right length for her legs. "Just walk the cloverleaf pattern right now. Follow the lines I made in the dirt."

Climbing into the saddle, Taylor signaled Mandy to walk toward the barrels. The gray mare was smaller but wider than Prince Albert, and it took Taylor a moment to adjust to the difference. In some ways, Mandy was easier to ride. "Smart girl," Taylor praised Mandy, who walked the course without even having to be told what to do. "She's a fast learner," Taylor said to the others.

"I know. She's great that way," Daphne agreed.

"Try it at a jog now," Eric suggested.

At the faster gait, Taylor got a sense of the excitement of the event. Sitting forward, she flicked the reins, moving Mandy into a lope.

"All right! That's it!" Eric cheered her on. "Way to go!"

Taylor's heart raced with the thrill of turning sharply around each barrel. She cleared the first one, and then the second. Gripping Mandy with her legs, she leaned forward in the saddle, giving Mandy more rein so she could stretch her neck out, driving the horse faster.

"Look at her go!" Mercedes cheered.

Taylor was coming around the third barrel when, suddenly, Shafir was right in her path. She had been standing calmly a minute ago, but now she was galloping headlong toward the barrels.

"Shafir! No!" Mercedes shouted.

"She wants to play!" Daphne cried.

"Whoa!" Taylor pulled back on Mandy's reins to keep from colliding with Shafir, but the mare couldn't stop in time. To avoid the crash, Mandy veered sharply to the right.

Taylor lost her grip. In the next second she was sailing through the air.

Taylor lay on her living room couch with a bag of ice wrapped in a kitchen towel on her right ankle. Travis sat in a straight-back chair beside her playing Mario Kart with the sound off. "Was I asleep?" she asked him.

"For a little bit," Travis reported, still playing. "How do you feel?"

"My ankle's freezing."

Travis rolled his eyes. "But does it hurt?"

Moving carefully, Taylor tried to rotate her ankle. A stab of sharp pain made her cringe. "Yes! Yes, it hurts."

Jennifer came in with a fresh pack of ice in a dry towel. "It's not too badly swollen," she remarked as she took away the old pack. "How does the rest of you feel?"

"I'm fine," Taylor insisted. "You heard what the doctor in the emergency room said; it's only twisted."

Jennifer shut her eyes and breathed deeply. "Thank goodness," she said. "When Mrs. LeFleur called and said you'd been thrown — well, you can imagine. I immediately thought the worst."

"So did Mrs. LeFleur," Travis said, putting down the game control. "She was shaking when she came to the corral and saw you on the ground there. For a second I thought she was gonna faint."

Taylor remembered what Mr. Romano had told her about Jimmy LeFleur and how he'd never seen Jimmy or Mrs. LeFleur again after the accident.

"I don't know if you should ride anymore, Taylor," Jennifer said. "It's just too dangerous."

"Mom!" Taylor cried. "Don't say that!"

"You could have been hurt much more seriously," Jennifer insisted.

"Daphne said everybody falls eventually. You just have to get right back on," Taylor argued.

"You're not getting back on any time soon," Jennifer replied.

"Mom, please! Don't be like that. I'm fine!"

"Well, you're not riding again until that swelling goes down."

Taylor's shoulders sagged with relief. "That was a close one," she said quietly to Travis once Jennifer had gone back into the kitchen. "I'd die if she wouldn't let me ride again."

"You wouldn't die," Travis disagreed. "Besides, it was your fault."

"My fault?"

"Yeah, you were showing off for that Eric guy," Travis said, turning the Mario Kart game on again.

"I was not!" Taylor maintained indignantly, though Travis's words caused her some doubt. *Had* she been going too fast because she'd wanted to show Eric how well she could ride? Maybe Travis was right.

The doorbell rang and then the door opened immediately. A tall, lanky man dressed in oil-smeared coveralls walked into the house. "Hey, Dad," Taylor greeted her father, Steve Henry.

Taylor realized she was smiling from ear to ear and quickly adopted a less thrilled expression. She hadn't seen her dad in nearly a month, not since she'd gone down to the car repair place where he worked to plead with him to let her keep Prince Albert and Pixie. Back then he'd said he would come by to visit her at the house that week, but she'd known he wouldn't. In fact, she'd seen very little of him since the divorce.

"How's my little bronco buster?" Steve asked. "Your mom says you took a tumble while you were Wild West rodeo riding."

"It's not a joke, Steve," Jennifer said, coming back into the living room.

"I know. But she looks okay to me."

"Her ankle's swollen," Jennifer told him.

Steve walked around the couch to get a look at Taylor's ankle. "Hey there, Travis," he said, slapping Travis's palm as he went. "I think she'll live," he said to Jennifer. "You went to the hospital, right?"

Steve bent to sit on the end of the couch, but Jennifer

put a hand up to stop him. "Not in those greasy clothes, please. I'll get a towel for you."

"Whatever," Steve replied, standing.

Once Jennifer set down the towel, he took a seat.

"Mrs. LeFleur said she remembered you," Taylor told him. "She called you little Stevie Henry."

Her dad grinned. "Yeah, that's what they called me back then, Little Stevie, because I was a shrimp. Thank goodness I grew in high school."

"Guys grow a lot in high school, don't they?" Travis asked. Travis was the same height as Taylor. For the first time, she realized he was worried about growing taller.

"Yep. That's the average time for it," Steve confirmed. He patted the bit of excess belly fat he carried under his mechanics jumpsuit. "Nobody calls me Little Stevie anymore."

"I wonder if Mrs. LeFleur would recognize you," Taylor said.

"Is she the one running the place now?" Steve asked.

Taylor nodded.

"That makes sense; it was her uncle's. She used to give lessons and take out trail rides. She was a blue-ribbon jumper, too. I remember that they had all her ribbons and medals displayed in the front office. She had a ton of them."

"Did Mrs. Ross ever come to the ranch?" Taylor asked.

"That rich woman?"

"Yeah."

"I don't know. I wouldn't have known what she looked like."

Taylor pulled herself up onto her elbows. "Did you know Mrs. LeFleur's son, a kid named Jimmy LeFleur, when you were there?"

Steve wrinkled his forehead and sat forward as he tried to remember. "Was he a blond kid?"

"I don't know."

"Oh, wow!" he said, sitting back in his chair. "I do remember him. He wound up in a wheelchair after a bad riding accident."

"A wheelchair! Did he ever get better?" Taylor asked.

"I don't know. I only saw him once after that, and then he and his mom never came back again."

Chapter 8

Taylor spent Tuesday on the couch with her ankle propped on a pillow. The TV played a game show as she helped her mother prepare for a luncheon she was catering. Taylor peeled long ribbons of carrots to decorate a salad. "I'm supposed to be injured, you know," Taylor complained to Jennifer. "Shouldn't I be resting?"

Jennifer came out of the kitchen holding a large wooden bowl filled with hard-boiled eggs. "Okay, then turn off the TV, and you can go lie down in your room."

Taylor's ankle still throbbed, but she wasn't in enough pain to simply do nothing. "Why don't I just sit here and read a book," she suggested, aiming for a compromise.

"If you're well enough to read you can peel a carrot," Jennifer replied. "Come on. I need some help."

"But my fingers are turning orange," Taylor grumbled, holding her hand up to show off what she considered a definite orangey tinge.

"They look fine to me. Keep peeling," Jennifer insisted. "You can read once I leave."

With a sigh, Taylor went back to work. What she was trying to accomplish was tricky. On the one hand, she was downplaying her injury so her mother would let her go back to the ranch by Wednesday. On the other hand, Taylor wanted to act like she was hurt enough that Jennifer wouldn't put her to work.

"You can't have it both ways, you know," Jennifer said, making Taylor wonder if her mother had actually read her mind.

A short, athletic woman with brown hair in a blunt bob cut to her chin came in the front door. "Have what both ways?" asked Claire Black, Jennifer's best friend since childhood. Claire was an animal rehabilitator, which meant that she went out to rescue lost, abandoned, or injured animals. Taylor had often gone with Claire on rescue calls, which came from an individual or the county sheriff. It was on one such rescue that they came upon Prince Albert and Pixie abandoned in a small private stable by a divorcing couple who, they learned from neighbors, had simply driven away.

"Oh, it's nothing," Taylor told her.

Claire's brindle-coated pit bull, Bunny, trotted up to Taylor and licked her hand. Then she moved down to Taylor's ankle and sniffed before sitting on the floor, as though guarding the injured ankle. "Look! She can tell that's where I'm hurt," Taylor said to Claire.

"Animals know stuff like that," Claire agreed. "How do you feel?"

"It still hurts," Taylor admitted.

"Are you scared to ride again?" Claire asked.

Taylor thought about it. "I don't think so," she said truthfully. "Daphne says everyone falls."

"That's why you wear helmets. Let me go see what your mom needs help doing," Claire said, heading toward the kitchen.

Taylor went back to her peeling, but after a minute her cell phone tone signaled that she was receiving a text message. It was from a number she didn't recognize.

R U OK? CAN I C U AFTER SKOOL? ERIC

Taylor's breath stuck in her throat.

Eric wanted to visit her . . . here, in her house?

It was either too good to be true — or it was a total disaster. Taylor wasn't sure which.

Her small farmhouse-style home had been built in 1821. It had low ceilings and wide-plank floors. It was antique, but not in a fancy way. And since her mother had started working so hard on her catering business, it had become a bit on the messy side, too.

But Eric wanted to come see her. It was too exciting! How could she say no?

"Mom!" Taylor called. "Mom! Can Eric come over after school?"

"Eric who?" Jennifer shouted back from the kitchen.

Taylor tried to think of Eric's last name, but she didn't remember ever having heard it. "I don't know. He's the guy from down at the ranch I told you about."

"Okay. I guess it's all right."

Claire walked into the living room. "I'll be here while your mother is at the luncheon," she said. "Does Travis know you have a new boyfriend?"

"Travis isn't my boyfriend," Taylor insisted. "It's not like that."

"Are you sure?" Claire asked in a teasing voice.

"Yes! I'm sure."

"So this Eric *is* your boyfriend?" Claire checked.

"No! He's not my boyfriend, either. I don't have a boyfriend."

Claire grinned with laughter in her eyes. "Whatever you say."

"Neither of them is my boyfriend," Taylor insisted.

"I feel like it's all my fault," Eric said. He was sitting in a kitchen chair beside the couch. Taylor had done her best to brush her hair to a shine and had arranged it carefully on her pillow the moment she heard the front doorbell ring.

"It wasn't your fault. You told me to take it slow. I just never expected Shafir to run out like that."

"Mercedes was supposed to be keeping an eye on her," Eric said.

"And she'd just finished giving me a big talk about not letting Prince Albert get away from me. She forgot how much Shafir likes to play," Taylor said. "She never expected Shafir to break out like that, either."

"It could have been a lot worse if Mandy hadn't veered off in time," Eric said. "If you guys had crashed" — his shoulders shuddered — "I don't even want to think about it. That's probably why Mrs. LeFleur got so upset. She knew what could have happened."

"I heard that her son got stuck in a wheelchair because of a riding accident," Taylor told him.

"That stinks. Have you ever met him?"

"No. She's never mentioned him, either."

"I wonder if he still rides," Eric said.

"I don't know."

The doorbell rang, and Claire came out of the kitchen to answer. "Are you expecting anyone else?" she asked Taylor.

"No."

Travis walked into the room behind Claire. "Hey, Taylor, how are you —" He cut himself short when he saw Eric.

"Hey, Travis," Eric said.

"I didn't know you had company," Travis said to Taylor. "I should have told you I was coming over."

"That's all right. Come and sit down," Taylor said.

Why did she suddenly feel guilty? She wasn't doing anything wrong.

"I'm going to go," Travis said.

"But you just got here," Taylor pointed out.

"I have something to do. I just remembered," Travis said.

Taylor could always tell when Travis was lying, but this time she wasn't sure. He seemed to be telling the truth, but what could he have to do?

"I'm going to school tomorrow," she told Travis. "My dad brought me a cane to lean on. So I'll see you on the bus, okay?"

Travis turned to Eric. "Taylor and I always sit together on the bus. Always."

An uneasy silence arose in the room.

Claire broke the tension by walking in holding a bag of pretzels and popping it with a small bang. "Anybody hungry?" she asked.

"No, but if you have an apple, I'll take it," Travis said. "I'm going down to Wildwood to check on Prince Albert and Pixie. I'll make sure they're fed and that someone turns them out for a while. I'd do it myself, but Prince Albert hates guys."

"Tell me about it," Eric said with a laugh.

Taylor was surprised to discover that Travis actually did have something he intended to do. She'd been sure he was just making an excuse to leave. Maybe he'd just thought of it.

"Thanks so much, Travis," she said. "I really appreciate that."

"You don't have to go down there," Eric told Travis. "Mercedes has them in the pasture, and she'll feed them. I already checked."

"How could you have done that already? We just got out of school," Travis said.

"The Johnson School gets out before PV," Eric reminded him. "So I got there before you did."

Chapter 9

Y ou didn't have to run off like that yesterday. Do you not like Eric or something?" Taylor asked Travis on the school bus Wednesday morning. Bored of sitting on the couch — and of peeling vegetables — Taylor had managed to hobble onto the bus with the aid of the cane her father had brought her, even though each step hurt.

"He acts like he's so great just because he goes to that fancy Johnson School," Travis replied.

"I think he's nice," Taylor insisted.

Travis made a sort of choking noise in his throat. "Yeah, like, no kidding!" he scoffed. "Anyone can see that. That's why you can hardly walk right now. You were showing off."

"I was *not* showing off in front of Eric the other day!" Taylor insisted firmly.

"Yeah, sure."

"Daphne says everyone falls sooner or later."

"Everyone who shows off falls."

"No! Not just show-offs — everyone falls!" Taylor stated. "And I wasn't showing off!"

"Whatever," Travis said again as he took a Batman comic from his pack and began to flip through it.

Despite her private doubts, Taylor would never admit to Travis that she might have, indeed, been showing off. But why not tell the truth? Couldn't she simply say that Eric was really cute and she wanted him to like her? It wasn't as if Travis was her boyfriend. Normally, she told him everything. Why was this so different?

Travis was not looking up from his comic, so Taylor slid her copy of the Hobby Horse catalog from her pack and perused the Western riding show apparel. Although she admired the formal English-style outfits with their starched white shirts, tailored jackets, and domed velvet helmets — which were also represented toward the back of this catalog — she thought the Western gear was much more fun. Taylor wore a helmet at Wildwood Stables, but not one as nice as these, and she liked the sparkly show shirts.

"I could see you wearing that," Travis said, pointing to a smiling brunette modeling a yellow-and-black rhinestone-studded shirt, a black cowgirl hat, and fringed chaps. "You're the cowgirl type."

Taylor smiled at him, relieved their argument about Eric was over. "Really? I could see me wearing it, too. Are you going to help out with the games event?"

"Yeah, I guess so," Travis replied, closing his comic.

"I hope this ankle is better in enough time so I can participate in the games. I've got about two weeks. That should be enough time. I am so looking forward to this."

"It'll be better," Travis assured her. "When you want to do something you don't let anything get in your way."

"You make me sound so tough," Taylor commented.

"No, just determined," Travis replied. "It's a good thing."

During her lunch period, Taylor got permission to put up flyers announcing the game event at Wildwood Stables. Mrs. LeFleur had taken a photo of the front sign and written an announcement that told anyone who was interested in participating to call the ranch. Pixie would provide pony rides, and there would be refreshments and games for little kids. Mercedes and Daphne were posting the flyers at the high school, and they adorned the walls of local businesses where Mrs. LeFleur had already been.

Taylor was tacking a flyer to the bulletin board outside the main office when she realized Plum was standing behind her. Forcing a smile to her lips, Taylor turned. "Hey," she greeted Plum.

"Nobody's going to trailer a horse all the way over to Wildwood for this stupid thing," Plum stated.

Taylor's nostrils flared slightly as she drew in a calming breath. "We only need a few people to compete. Everyone else can watch," she replied in a voice she hoped was even and friendly. "Daphne has already talked to some of her friends from the high school who might be interested."

"*Might* be," Plum echoed pointedly.

"Maybe we could get Shafir ready in time for you to ride her," Taylor suggested.

"*I* could do it if you all would let me train her *my* way."

In that case, Shafir might be dead by the day of the games event, Taylor thought. "It's more fun if we all work together," she said brightly, then turned and hobbled to class.

Taylor wasn't able to ride her bike to the ranch so her mother drove her. "You are *not* to ride today, do you hear me?" Jennifer demanded. "Do you understand?"

"I understand. I hope Prince Albert understands, though."

"He'll just have to," Jennifer insisted. "I don't know why you even had to come here today. You should be resting."

"There are other things I need to do besides ride. For one thing, Dana has a therapeutic lesson today."

Jennifer pulled to a stop outside the main building. Dana, Lois, and Alice were already in the corral with Prince Albert and Pixie.

A sudden anxiety grabbed hold of Taylor. Why was Prince Albert saddled? Was Dana going to try to ride Prince Albert today?

Chapter 10

From her perch on the top rung of the corral fence, Taylor watched the scene before her through the lens of the lightweight, handheld video camera. Dana was leading Prince Albert through a small obstacle course set up in the corral. The reliable quarter horse walked in between two benches, around three orange cones, and across a platform that had been propped up on planks to create a low bridge. Taylor's worries had faded once she realized Dana was just leading Prince Albert, not trying to mount him yet.

Pixie had been hitched to the fence, probably to keep her from following Prince Albert through the course. The small pony watched intently as Prince Albert walked steadily along. Dana coached Prince Albert and some-times used the lunge whip as a gentle guide.

Dana beamed proudly, as she always did while work-ing with Prince Albert. She was no longer the sullen, moody girl she often seemed to be when she first drove in with her mother, Alice, at the start of each class.

When the obstacle course was successfully completed, Dana was radiant. "He does what I say. He's my friend," she announced jubilantly.

Lois, Dana's teacher, leaned close to the girl. Taylor zoomed in with the camera. "Dana, would you like to try to ride Prince Albert today?" Lois asked.

Taylor nearly dropped the camera as she pulled in an alarmed breath. Prince Albert was not ready to take on another rider.

Alice, who had been standing near the gate, watch-ing, hurried to them with an anxious expression. "Do you really think she's ready for that?" she asked Lois.

"We'll just walk around the corral," Lois replied. "She'll be fine."

Taylor quickly switched off the camera and lowered herself gingerly from the top rung of the fence, landing on her good foot. She hopped toward Lois as fast as she could.

Taylor hadn't expected this to happen so soon. She had hoped that by the time Dana was ready to ride Prince Albert, he would be agreeable to being ridden. "Why not let Dana ride Pixie?" Taylor suggested. "Dana is petite, and Pixie is probably a better size for her."

"Would you rather ride Pixie, the pony?" Lois checked with Dana. "She's nice, too."

Dana folded her arms and stared down at her riding shoes. She shook her head, tossing her blonde curls. "Pixie is not my friend. Prince Albert is my friend."

"Pixie can be your friend, too," Taylor coaxed Dana. "Want to pet her mane? It's nice and soft."

"No! No! No! No!" Dana shouted.

Lois smiled softly. "I guess she doesn't want to."

"I guess not, but sometimes Prince Albert is funny about new people riding him," Taylor said.

"Funny, in what way?" Lois asked.

"Like . . . sometimes he doesn't let a new person get in the saddle," Taylor admitted with a sheepish grin. She felt guilty about using the word *sometimes* when the truth was that Prince Albert had *never* let anyone other than Taylor in the saddle, at least not since Taylor had owned him.

"Why didn't you tell me that before?" Lois asked.

"Actually, I did," Taylor said. "Dana insisted on working only with Prince Albert. Remember, you tried to start her on Mandy, but Dana wouldn't have any horse but Prince Albert. We've been working with him, but he's not ready for her to ride. I'm pretty sure I mentioned the problem at the time."

Narrowing her eyes thoughtfully, Lois nodded. "I remember now. You did mention it. Sorry."

"It's okay."

Lois looked at Prince Albert, over at Dana, and then turned her attention back to Taylor. "He seems very relaxed with Dana. Why don't we see if he'll let her up on his back?" she suggested.

"We could try," Taylor allowed, although she didn't feel hopeful about the outcome.

"He doesn't nip or rear, or anything dangerous like that, does he?" Alice asked.

"No," Taylor replied. He hadn't done anything of that sort before, and Taylor really hoped he wouldn't start now.

Dana was resting her body against Prince Albert's side, tenderly rubbing his coat. Prince Albert had swung his head around and was watching her. "They look pretty comfortable with each other," Lois noted. "Let's give it a try."

Taking hold of his reins, Lois led Prince Albert out of the corral and brought him alongside the picnic bench beneath the big maple. Dana and Alice followed her out of the corral. "Taylor, do you have the camera ready?" Lois asked. "This is going to be an important moment."

Still holding the camera, Taylor switched it back on. "Ready," she confirmed.

Taylor's mind raced with thoughts of all the things that could go wrong. "Don't let him step on you," she warned Lois. "If he doesn't want a rider to get in the saddle, he sometimes moves to the side at the last second."

"Thanks for the warning," Lois replied. "Keep filming."

"Okay," Taylor said, training the video camera on Lois and Dana.

Alice had hurried to her car and returned with a black school helmet that she put on Dana, making sure it was buckled on securely.

Lois helped Dana up onto the picnic bench.

"Please, Albert, please," Taylor whispered. "Let her ride you."

Instructing Dana to swing her leg across, Lois guided her into the saddle.

Prince Albert swung his head around to look at Taylor. His dark eyes questioned her. *Is this all right? Do you mind?*

Taylor held the camera to her side and nodded reassuringly. "It's okay," she said gently. She hoped he could understand her expression as well as she could read his. They were still best friends. She needed to communicate that so he wouldn't worry. "I'm proud of you. Good boy," she told him softly.

Prince Albert neighed, and Taylor felt sure it was his response.

"I'm on a horse!" Dana cried joyfully when she was seated. "I'm riding a horse!"

Lifting the camera again, Taylor filmed Dana's reaction and then trained the video camera on Prince Albert. She stayed focused on her horse while Lois led him back into the corral with Dana in the saddle.

"No problem," Lois said to Taylor. "He's doing really well."

"Yeah, he's great," Taylor agreed, still filming. It was only when the view through the lens looked blurry that she realized there were tears in her eyes — tears of happiness and pride.

Chapter 11

Hello, Wildwood Stables ... You're interested in the rodeo? Great!"

By the end of the afternoon, Taylor's ankle had begun to ache, so Mrs. LeFleur assigned her to answer phones in the main office. It was turning out to be a much livelier assignment than Taylor had expected.

"Yes, you can trailer her horse here," Taylor told a woman who had called inquiring about how her daughter could participate. "Where is the horse currently boarded? By himself on your property? Well, that's not really good for the horse. Horses are herd animals and like to be with other horses. You might want to consider boarding him here where he'd have some company. You can check out the stables when you come for the rodeo. Okay, see you then. Bye."

"Hey, what a saleswoman!" Eric cheered as he came into the office.

"Thanks, I'm trying! Look at this!" Taylor handed him a yellow legal pad on which she'd listed the names and numbers of all the people who had called about the games event. "And Maria's Pizzeria is giving us pies at half price so we can sell them to earn money," Taylor added.

"Why are they being so generous?" Eric asked.

"Maria said she liked Mrs. LeFleur's uncle, and she's glad to see the place reopen," Taylor said. "Plus, Maria's is the closest pizzeria. If the ranch gets busy, our riders will go there afterward."

"Mmm, a smart businesswoman, too," Eric proclaimed as he dropped into the couch to study the legal pad.

"What are you working on today?" Taylor asked.

"Daphne, Mercedes, and I found some stuff in the equipment shed. We're practicing a game called poles where you have to ride through the poles without touching them."

"Is it hard to do?"

Eric nodded. "It takes practice. Are you going to be able to ride later?"

"Not today. I promised my mother I wouldn't."

Mercedes passed the door, leading Shafir on a line attached to the Arabian's rope harness. "Plum's here to work with her. Want to help?" she asked, stopping by the open door.

"Can't," Taylor replied. "Phone duty."

"Okay. Don't worry. I'll stay close to her."

Taylor swiveled around to look out the window. Plum stood by the corral gate with her arms folded impatiently, waiting for Shafir to be delivered to her. "Poor Shafir," Taylor commented.

"Why do you say that?" Eric asked.

Taylor turned back toward him with a sigh. "Because he's being leased by that Plum Mason, and she is the worst."

"The worst what?"

"The worst horse trainer; the worst snob in the school; the worst human being on the planet — just the plain out worst." Taylor told Eric about Plum's history of horse deaths. "So we're all acting as if we like her so she'll let us stay close enough to protect Shafir from her."

"Clever plan," Eric commented. "So, you say this Plum is really horrible?" he said jokingly.

"Totally awful," Taylor replied with a smile.

Without warning, Plum appeared at the office door.

Taylor and Eric exchanged quick, worried glances. Had she heard them talking?

"I want to put a real halter on that horse," Plum demanded. "That rope thing is ridiculous."

"I picked it because it's light, and Shafir isn't used to being tacked up," Taylor said, defending her choice.

"Okay, so she's already spent a whole day with it, now it's time to move on. Where's the tack room? I'll pick a better halter out myself," Plum said.

"It's right behind you," Taylor told her.

Plum glanced at Eric as if noticing him for the first time. "What are you doing here? Why aren't you over at Westheimer's?"

"It's not my day to work there."

Taylor's eyes darted between Eric and Plum. Did they know each other?

"I'm working on the rodeo games," Eric added.

"For that stupid show?"

"It's not stupid," Eric insisted. "Too bad you can't ride Shafir or you could be in it."

"Oh, puh-lease. I only ride English." Plum turned toward the tack room. "*This* is it?" she asked. "It should be called the tacky room. What a dump!"

Taylor ignored Plum; she was too stunned to speak. Raising her eyebrows and tilting her head, she looked pointedly at Eric.

"Plum's my cousin," Eric answered Taylor's unspoken question.

Taylor ran a brush through Pixie's mane while she waited for Mrs. LeFleur, who was giving her a ride home, to finish in the office. "I'm going to bring some hair detangler for you," she told Pixie. "How do you get so knotted up?"

From his adjacent stall, Prince Albert whinnied.

"That's my good boy," Taylor praised him.

Mrs. LeFleur came down the center aisle with her purse slung over her shoulder, ready to leave. "I heard that his highness the prince had a breakthrough this afternoon," she remarked.

"Yes, he did!" Taylor agreed.

"Do you think he'll let anyone other than Dana and you ride him now?"

"I don't know," Taylor admitted. "It's a good start, though, don't you think?"

"An excellent start," Mrs. LeFleur said. "We can have Daphne or Mercedes try him tomorrow. How are you all doing with Shafir?"

"I think she's making progress. She wanted to play with us the other day. If she wants to play badly enough she might let someone saddle her."

"I saw Plum trying to put a leather halter on Shafir today," Mrs. LeFleur said. "She was having a great deal of difficulty, though. The rope halter is probably better."

"I tried to tell her that." Taylor put her brush back in the ranch's curry kit and closed it. "A lot of people called about the rodeo games," she commented, eager to get off the topic of Plum.

"I know. We will be extremely busy until next Saturday. Could you come tomorrow even though it's not your regular day?"

"Sure!"

"We'll have all sorts of horses here, food, events —

such fun. And listen to this: I called Channel Twelve news and they're sending a reporter to cover our event."

"We're going to be on TV?"

"Isn't it exciting?"

"Very exciting," Taylor agreed.

"So why don't you seem happier?" Mrs. LeFleur asked.

"I'm happy," Taylor insisted.

"Oh, no, you're not. I can see it on your face. Something happened."

"You're good, Mrs. LeFleur," Taylor said as she came out of Pixie's stall, locking the door. "What happened is I made an idiot of myself in front of Eric. Did you know he was Plum's cousin?"

"Really? No. I had no idea."

"His name is Eric Mason."

"Oh, dear. Can I assume you made some uncomplimentary remark about Plum?" Mrs. LeFleur guessed.

Taylor threw her arms wide in distress. "I told him Plum was the worst person on the planet!"

Mrs. LeFleur let out a short blast of laughter before resuming her serious expression. "Oh, my. How did he respond to that?"

"He said he knew she was a brat." Taylor lifted her cane off the stall door. It felt good to take some weight off her bad ankle.

"So, it was all right?" Mrs. LeFleur asked.

They began walking together up the aisle toward the main center sliding doors. "I don't know," Taylor said. "She's his cousin, after all; though I can still hardly believe it. They're so different. I was so embarrassed."

As they walked outside, Taylor was amazed to discover it was nearly dark. They got into Mrs. LeFleur's green compact car. "We all make mistakes," Mrs. LeFleur said consolingly as she started the engine.

"He probably hates me now," Taylor muttered.

"Does it matter so much what he thinks?"

"I guess not," Taylor said. But even as she said it, she realized it did matter — to her, anyway.

Chapter 12

By Thursday, the swelling in Taylor's ankle was gone, though it still hurt if she bumped it. As she stood before her locker and got out her notebooks, Taylor scanned the hallway, looking for Plum. Had Eric said anything to her? Taylor wondered if she should apologize to Plum or just pretend she'd never said anything at all to Eric.

Really, why should she consider apologizing to Plum? The two girls openly disliked each other. It wasn't as though anything Eric told his cousin would come as a big surprise to Plum.

Only . . . maybe it would.

Was it possible that Plum really thought they liked her down at Wildwood Stables? If she believed that, it was understandable. Daphne, Mercedes, and Taylor had done their best to convince Plum of their friendship. *Things should be different at Wildwood Stables.* Taylor had said so herself.

Travis came down the hall and stopped at Taylor's locker. "Hey, home girl. What's shak-a-lackin'?"

Taylor squinted at him quizzically. "Why are you talking like that?"

"Just felt like it," Travis explained with a grin.

"Travis, do you think it's mean that we're pretending to like Plum down at the ranch, even though we don't?"

"Definitely. It's like something Plum would do."

"That's cold," Taylor told him. "I'm not like Plum."

"Not in any other way," Travis said with a shrug. "You asked me what I thought, so . . ."

"Maybe it *is* mean," Taylor answered her own question.

"But it's Plum," Travis reminded her.

"I know. And it's for a good cause — to protect Shafir."

"So, what's the problem?" Travis asked.

"It just feels wrong all of a sudden," Taylor admitted. "There could be a more honest way to protect Shafir."

"You could try to really like Plum," Travis suggested, "try to see her good side."

Taylor and Travis looked at each other and let the impact of what Travis had just said sink in. "Naw," they both said at once, shaking their heads.

"Not possible," said Travis.

"Definitely not," Taylor agreed.

Taylor felt so embarrassed by what had happened with Eric that she seriously considered not going to the ranch that afternoon. But she had promised Mrs. LeFleur she would.

Her ankle felt close to fine and Jennifer wasn't home to object, so she went back to riding her bike down to the ranch.

As soon as she leaned her bike against the maple, Daphne hurried over to her. "Come and check this out," she insisted, pulling Taylor by the arm. "You won't believe it."

"What is it?"

"You'll see."

Daphne led Taylor around to the side paddock just across from the outside stalls. In the middle, Plum sat on top of Shafir. The only tack was the rope harness and a horse pad.

"How did you get on her?" Daphne asked Plum, straddling the paddock fence.

"I was working with her in here and she started grazing near the fence, so I ran in and grabbed a horse pad, climbed the fence, and sat down," Plum explained triumphantly.

"Did she give you a hard time?" Daphne asked.

Plum shook her head. "She just finally got used to me, I suppose."

"Nice work," Taylor said. But instantly she doubted her own motives. Was she being sincere or phony? No. She was being real — it *was* impressive that Plum had managed to get Shafir to cooperate.

"I told you I could do it," Plum replied.

"Yeah, because she tried it our way instead of her way," Daphne murmured under her breath.

"True, but at least she was willing to do that," Taylor replied softly.

"You're right," Daphne agreed.

Later that afternoon, Taylor decided that, while still a bit tender and bruised, she felt well enough to ride. She was practicing quick stops with Prince Albert in the front corral as Pixie watched from the side. She had just reined Prince Albert to a halt when Rick drove in towing a horse trailer. Eric hurried out of the front seat and unloaded Jojo from the back. He walked him into the main building without glancing Taylor's way.

A sickening lump formed in Taylor's stomach. Was Eric ignoring her?

A second trailer pulled in, and Mrs. LeFleur came out to meet it. "We have a new horse boarding with us," she called to Taylor. "Come see."

Taylor rode to the fence near the trailer with Pixie meeting Prince Albert there. Mrs. LeFleur met her on the opposite side of the fence.

A bald man with a round belly opened up the back of

the trailer. Out stepped a white gelding with black spots and a black-and-white mane and tail. "His name is Cody and he's a Colorado Ranger," the man told them. "He's going to be a Christmas present for my daughter when she comes home from college at the end of the semester."

"I know this horse!" Taylor realized. "I rode him over at Ross River Ranch when I was there with Daphne. It was the same day we met Shafir. He belonged to Mrs. Ross's daughter."

"She sold Leslie's horse!" Mrs. LeFleur cried, aghast.

Taylor looked at Mrs. LeFleur curiously. How did she know the name of Mrs. Ross's daughter? Did she know Cody, too? "Mrs. Ross said her daughter never rides him anymore," Taylor explained.

"Still, Cody was a gift to her daughter."

She did know the horse!

The man stepped toward them. "If anybody here wants to ride Cody, I'd like him to get the exercise," he said. "My daughter will be away at college a lot for the next couple of years. She'll only be home on breaks."

"May I take him out for trail rides and use him for lessons?" Mrs. LeFleur asked.

"Sure thing. I think he'd love that." The man shook hands with Mrs. LeFleur. "I'm Ed Myers, pleased to meet you."

"I've ridden him; he's a really well-trained horse," Taylor mentioned.

"I'm glad to hear that. It's what Mrs. Ross told me. Personally, I wouldn't know," Ed replied.

Mercedes came out from the side of the main building. When she saw the trailer, her eyes lit up and she ran over. "This is our new boarder, isn't it? Oh, he's gorgeous!"

"Meet Cody. Ride him as much as you like."

Mercedes' jaw dropped and her eyes went wide. "Are you kidding?"

"The only time you can't ride him is when my daughter is home from college and wants to ride."

"We're holding a games event here next Saturday. Can I ride him in that?" Mercedes asked.

"Is she a good rider?" Ed asked Mrs. LeFleur.

"Excellent," Mrs. LeFleur confirmed.

"Then sure thing."

Mercedes jumped up and punched the air joyfully. "Yes! Yes! I'm going to be in the games event! I was dying to, but I had no horse. Now I have one!"

"Don't worry, Ed," Mrs. LeFleur said. "Mercedes is normally a very sensible girl. She'll take good care of Cody."

"Can I tack him up now?" Mercedes asked.

"I bet he'd love to be ridden," Ed agreed.

Eric rode Jojo out of the main building. "Meet everyone over in the paddock. Today we're practicing stalls," he announced.

Mercedes led Cody toward the main building. "Wait for me," she shouted to Eric. "I'll be there as soon as I get Cody saddled."

"Come on, Taylor," Eric shouted with a wave of his arm. "We can get started."

Taylor's face broke into a wide smile. He wasn't angry or giving her the silent treatment, after all.

With new excitement, Taylor headed Prince Albert to the corral gate with Pixie behind. Mrs. LeFleur opened it for her, and Taylor got into step beside Eric.

They walked together without speaking until they were clear of the main building and could see the paddock across from the outdoor stalls.

Plum was there posting up and down, riding Shafir at a steady trot. Taylor had to admit that Plum seemed pretty competent in her riding style. Plum also appeared to be the picture of an expert rider in her breeches, high boots, and domed velvet helmet.

"She's brought Shafir along fast," Taylor said.

"I know," Eric agreed. "She's set on entering the games event."

"She said she wasn't entering," Taylor reminded him.

"Plum changed her mind after I talked to her last night. She's determined to show everyone she's a better rider than you are."

Taylor's stomach clenched. "You told her what I said?" she asked, feeling sick. Even if Plum was horrible, Taylor didn't like the idea of hurting her feelings like that. "You know I feel badly about saying all that about her. Plus I had no idea she was your cousin."

"I didn't tell her any of that stuff. Besides, she knows you're just putting up with her for the sake of the horse."

"She does?" Taylor asked, surprised.

"Yeah, she thinks you don't trust her with Shafir."

"Then how come she's so worked up about beating me?" Taylor asked. "What did you say to her?"

"I said I thought you were a gutsy girl, the way you got thrown like that and didn't make a big deal over it."

"Thanks," Taylor said. "That's all you said?"

"No. I told her I thought you were a lot of fun . . . and cute."

Taylor's heart raced nervously as she looked at Eric, not knowing what to say next.

Prince Albert neighed and Taylor petted his neck. "I guess we should start practicing," she said, too flustered to say anything else.

Chapter 13

That night Taylor studied her image in the long mirror behind her bedroom door. Was she really cute? She'd never aspired to be cute; before today she had thought it was a dumb sort of word if it was used to describe someone over the age of six. Kittens and puppies were cute. Little kids were cute. But when Eric had described her as cute, she hadn't minded at all. In fact, thinking about it at that moment made her smile.

Turning her face to the right and then to the left, Taylor tried to see herself as Eric saw her. He'd said she was gutsy, fun — and cute. Was she? It seemed as though he must be talking about someone else — but he'd said it to her!

Did it mean he liked her — *liked* liked her?

Or did he simply think she was some sort of adorable, spunky, Annie Oakley–type cowgirl?

And, either way, why should it bother Plum so much?

Eric *must* have told Plum he *liked* liked her. That was the only reason Plum would be so bugged about it.

Taylor got into bed. Picking up her cell phone, she found a text message from Travis.

HOW WUZ RANCH 2DAY?

GOOD. PRACTICED GAMES.

She put the phone down but a reply tone sounded almost instantly.

ANYTHING ELSE HAPPN?

NOT RLY. G2G. NEED Z'S.

OK. C U LTR.

OK. NITE.

Taylor switched off her phone and pulled her covers up. She felt as if so much had happened, yet she couldn't tell Travis about it. The whole thing gave her a weird feeling. She didn't want to think about it so she hurried herself off to sleep.

On Friday afternoon, Eric planned to meet up with Mercedes, Daphne, Taylor, and Plum in the pasture. The girls arrived before he did, each on horseback: Daphne on Mandy, Mercedes on Cody, Taylor on Prince Albert with Pixie alongside, and Plum on Shafir.

"You got the leather halter on Shafir," Mercedes mentioned to Plum.

"Yes, it wasn't hard," Plum replied.

"Did you use the tips I gave you yesterday?" Mercedes asked.

Plum looked away from her. "Some of them. But Shafir was ready because she's taking to my training."

In a flicker, a look traveled from Mercedes to Daphne to Taylor. Plum could simply not admit that she was succeeding because of all the advice she was getting from Daphne and Mercedes.

"Who knows how to play bandanna snatch?" Eric called to them as he rode into the pasture on Jojo.

"I do," Daphne replied.

"Daphne showed me how to play, but I've only done it

once," Taylor answered. She pointed to Cody. "I was riding that guy at the time. Daphne, didn't you tell me Cody already knew the game?"

"He's played a bunch of times that I know of," Daphne agreed.

"What's the prize if we win these games?" Plum asked.

"Mrs. LeFleur is at the printer's having ribbons made up," Daphne told her. "They say Wildwood Stables on them."

Eric took a red bandanna from his back pocket and tucked it in the cheek strap of Jojo's bridle. "Daphne and I will show you how to do it, and as you get the idea, you can join in."

Eric flicked his reins, and Jojo loped away into the pasture. In a minute, Daphne rode off after him. Taylor could tell neither of them was riding full out since this was more of a demonstration than a real competition. Daphne directed Mandy alongside Eric. As she rode, she reached out and pulled the bandanna from Jojo's strap.

Daphne raised the bandanna triumphantly in her hand. "Score!" she sang out. Tucking it into Mandy's bridle, she rode a wide circle in the field.

Shafir whinnied and gave a low buck, kicking out her back legs.

"Whoa!" Plum shouted.

"She's just excited," Taylor defended the Arabian. "She saw this game when Daphne and I were playing, and she wanted to join in so badly."

Plum glowered at Taylor. "Well, now she *can* play," she said, leaning forward. "And she'll win!" Plum kicked Shafir's sides as she loosened her reins. "Giddyap!"

Shafir took off fast, galloping toward Mandy.

Without even thinking, Taylor sat forward in the saddle, pressing her heels into the stirrups, and flicked her loosened reins. "Come on, boy, let's get 'em," she shouted, gripping Prince Albert's sides with her knees.

Prince Albert headed out fast in the direction of the other horses. Taylor stayed forward, pressing Prince Albert on faster and faster.

From the corner of her eye, Taylor saw Mercedes ride Cody out. Soon all the riders were galloping in pursuit of Daphne and Mandy.

Daphne stayed in front of them. Taylor knew she and Prince Albert couldn't outride these more experienced competitors. The only way to win this game would be to outmaneuver the other riders.

Peeling off from the group, Taylor galloped in a circle as if to cut Daphne and Mandy off. Seeing this, Daphne veered right. Plum was the first one to follow her out, riding toward her at a diagonal.

Mandy and Shafir were riding neck and neck, thundering across the pasture. Plum reached forward, poised to grab the bandanna.

To break the deadlock, Daphne pulled Mandy into a quick left turn, which put her directly in Taylor's path. Taylor shouted, putting on a burst of speed. In minutes she'd reached Mandy and snatched the bandanna!

Taylor's heart hammered as she twirled the bandanna in the air, hooting with victory.

"All right!" Eric cheered.

Mercedes and Daphne applauded. The only one not cheering was Plum, who was riding off to the other side of the pasture.

"Where are you going?" Daphne called after her.

"Shafir and I are going to work down in the paddock," she shouted back. "Shafir's a winner, and she's going to win this. But she has to work harder."

The girls looked at one another warily. "I'll go work with her," Mercedes volunteered, riding after her.

"You think she's going to be too hard on Shafir?" Eric asked.

"To be honest, yes," Taylor replied.

Eric nodded thoughtfully. "And she's determined to take home all the ribbons, too."

Taylor twirled the bandanna. "Well, she might not get her way this time."

Later that afternoon, Taylor was mucking out Pixie's stall with a rake when Mrs. LeFleur approached down the center aisle with Lois beside her. "Taylor, we need to talk to you," said Mrs. LeFleur when they were close.

Taylor leaned the rake against the wall. "What's up?"

"It's good news," said Lois. "The Rotary Club is sponsoring a horse show for children with special needs, and we've entered Dana in the Walk/Trot Division, which is the category with the most entrants."

"Cool," Taylor said. "Dana must be super excited about it."

"She's completely thrilled," Lois confirmed. "I've never

seen her so over the moon about anything. Working with Prince Albert in this short time has brought her out of her shell like nothing before. She's more focused, more social. I'm so pleased."

"Prince Albert is a really great horse," Taylor said, looking out of Pixie's stall to the next stall over, where the gelding stood watching them. Taylor petted Pixie's mane. "Pixie could tell you that. She's a big Prince Albert fan, aren't you, girl?"

Pixie realized all eyes were on her and sputtered.

"So what I came to talk to you about is using Prince Albert on that day. We'd pay the ranch, of course. We'd also need a horse handler, and we'd like to hire you for that job. We could pay you seventy-five dollars for the day."

"Wow," Taylor commented.

"You'd handle Prince Albert during the trip and lead Dana around the course. He was great with Dana the other day, but I'm sure he'd be most comfortable with you there. I don't want him to be scared and think we're taking him away from his home."

"That's true," Taylor agreed. "He might think that if we hauled him out of here in a trailer without me."

"So, is it a deal?" Lois asked.

"Sure, when is it?"

"Saturday."

"Tomorrow? I can do that."

"No, next Saturday," Lois corrected Taylor.

"Oh, dear," said Mrs. LeFleur.

"Next Saturday is our big games event," Taylor said. "I couldn't miss that."

"Oh, no," Lois said. "Dana will be so disappointed."

Taylor looked to Mrs. LeFleur for some kind of advice or help. What should she do?

"It's up to you, dear," Mrs. LeFleur answered the question in Taylor's eyes. "You have to decide."

Chapter 14

There will be other shows for Dana to be in," Travis said on Saturday morning, speaking over the banging of his hammer. They'd gotten to Wildwood early that morning because Mrs. LeFleur had asked Travis to build some wooden booths from which they could sell refreshments and raffle tickets.

"I know," Taylor said as she sat beside him under the maple and handed him another bunch of nails. "But there will be other game events for me to be in, too."

"There might not be if *this* game event isn't a success," Travis pointed out. "Isn't Mrs. LeFleur counting on this to raise money and bring in new customers?"

"Yes, but I have all this week to help her set up. I don't have to be there on the actual day. A lot of people have signed up to compete, and even more have called for directions so they can come down to watch. Plus there's another thing to think about."

"What's that?" Travis asked, resting his hammer on the wooden board beside him.

"Wildwood now has two horses to use for lessons, Mandy and Cody. I don't know yet if Prince Albert will let anyone but Dana and me ride him. If I don't keep Dana as a customer, then he'll just be taking up space at Wildwood, and Mrs. LeFleur can't afford that."

"Do you really think Dana and Lois would stop coming if you don't let them ride Prince Albert next weekend?" Travis questioned.

"Maybe they'd still come, but if Dana can be convinced to use another horse, she might stick with that horse afterward."

Just then, Alice's car pulled into the ranch with Dana in the passenger's seat beside her mother. Surprised to see them, Taylor stood, brushing off her jeans. "I didn't know you had a lesson today," she said to Alice as the woman got out of the car.

"We don't, but Dana wanted to visit Prince Albert," Alice explained. "I hope that's all right."

"Sure. He's in his stall right now."

Dana heard what Taylor had said and abruptly ran for the main building. "Don't run, Dana!" Alice called to her.

Dana slowed for three steps and then resumed her race into the building. "She just adores that horse," Alice said. "Children with autism find it so difficult to make social connections. And they can't always empathize with someone else's feelings, either. Even though Prince Albert is an animal and not a person, she's still connected with him. Working with Prince Albert has been a huge step in the right direction for her. When Lois suggested horse therapy, I admit that I was doubtful, but now I'm a total believer."

"She does seem happy when she's with him," Taylor observed.

"Happy, plus focused, self-confident, and in charge," Alice added. "Prince Albert is so good and patient with her. What a perfect horse for this kind of work."

"I could saddle him up and lead her around the corral," Taylor offered.

"Oh, would you? She would love that! Her helmet's in the trunk."

"Sure. I'll go tack him up."

In the main building, Taylor stopped at the tack room across from the office and picked up the light, all-purpose saddle she liked to use most, a bridle with a snaffle bit, and a saddle pad. Loading them all in the wheelbarrow parked in the corner, she wheeled them toward Prince Albert's stall.

In a minute, Taylor could see Dana at Prince Albert's stall, tenderly stroking his muzzle. Prince Albert had his head tipped down, enabling her small, delicate hands to reach him better. There was a gentle, unspoken communication between the little girl and the sturdy black quarter horse; somehow Taylor was sure of it.

Taylor came up on them quietly, not wanting to startle either one. "Hey," she said quietly, leaning toward Dana. "Would you like to ride him?"

Dana's eyes lit up and she nodded excitedly.

"Come on, you help me get him ready. I'll show you how," Taylor said, opening the stall door and leading Prince Albert out by his halter. "You stay right next to me.

You don't want to stand behind Prince Albert, do you understand that?"

Dana nodded. "He might kick me," she volunteered.

"That's right!" Taylor said, impressed. "How did you know?"

"I've been reading every book about horses. I'm learning a lot."

"Good for you!" Taylor praised Dana as she placed the saddle pad on Prince Albert's back. "This pad cushions Prince Albert's back. You're not very heavy, so I picked a lightweight pad."

At every stage, Taylor explained to Dana what she was doing, and the girl listened with rapt attention. After Taylor demonstrated how she adjusted the stirrups, she let Dana try the second stirrup. Dana was a quick learner and accomplished the task with ease.

Taylor clipped on a lead line and offered the other end to Dana. "You lead him out."

Dana reached for the line but then hesitated nervously.

"You can do it," Taylor encouraged her. "You led him in the corral."

"But what if he runs when I get him outside?" Dana asked.

"He won't run. He knows you're in charge. Plus, he likes you; he doesn't want to run away from you."

Smiling, Dana patted Prince Albert. Then she took the line from Taylor and began walking forward.

Taylor opened Pixie's stall to let her out.

"Does she always have to come?" Dana asked with a note of complaint.

"She likes to be with Prince Albert," Taylor replied. "She feels safe with him, I think. You don't want her to be scared, do you?"

Dana considered the question for a moment.

Taylor recalled what Alice had said about Dana's difficulty understanding what another person might be feeling. Could she sympathize with a pony's fears?

"No. I don't want her to be scared," Dana finally decided. "Pixie can come with Prince Albert."

"I'm sure she appreciates that you understand," Taylor said.

Outside, Alice put on Dana's black plastic school helmet. Taylor helped Dana mount from the picnic table and then walked her into the corral with Pixie trailing behind. "Look, Mommy. I'm riding!" Dana shouted to her mother as Taylor led her around, following the fence.

Alice waved back, smiling. "You're doing great!"

"I'm going to be in a riding contest with Prince Albert," Dana told Taylor.

"Are you excited?" Taylor asked.

Dana nodded. "And scared, too. But with Prince Albert there, I can do it."

Taylor looked up at Dana sitting so tall and proud in the saddle. When she turned back, Taylor saw Eric propped on the lower rail of the fence outside the corral waving to her. "Ready for some poles practice later?" he asked.

Taylor shook her head. "I'm not going to compete in the games."

"Why not?"

"I'll be with Dana and Prince Albert at the Rotary's special event."

Eric looked at Dana on horseback and then back over to Taylor. "Are you sure?" he asked doubtfully. "You were doing really well. You could have won some ribbons."

Taylor sighed wistfully. There was only one choice she could make and still feel good about herself — which meant there was really no choice at all.

"Yep," she said. "I'm sure."

Chapter 15

We have to get every stall ready with fresh hay. People aren't going to want to keep their horses in trailers all day, especially after they've participated in events," Mrs. LeFleur told Taylor on Monday afternoon. "Plus we want them to see how nice everything is so they'll want to board their horses here."

Taylor felt a little like Cinderella, sweeping the outside stalls with the sounds of thundering hoofbeats and peals of laughter in the background as the others practiced. Looking out to the empty paddock across from the stalls, she could glimpse her friends in the farther paddock where they were riding. Occasionally, she watched Eric on Jojo raise his hand and signal the riders to begin.

But an hour later, Mercedes and Daphne were with her, pitching hay into the stalls. Travis was also there, hammering down or pulling out any dangerous old nails that were protruding from the stalls.

"Plum is riding Shafir too hard," Mercedes complained.

"Did you say something to her?" Taylor asked.

"Yes, and she accused me of wanting her to slow down just so I can win the events," Mercedes revealed.

"That girl can really make you want to scream," Daphne remarked as she spread the hay in a stall.

"Ha!" Travis cried as he slammed a nail with a *bang*. He looked up and grinned. "It's fun to hit things while discussing Plum."

"That's terrible, Travis," Taylor scolded mildly, throwing a handful of hay at him.

Travis just shrugged and yanked out another nail with the claw end of his hammer.

"I'm glad we told Eric what we think of Plum's riding," Mercedes said. "I hope he talks to her."

"Plum doesn't listen to anybody," Daphne said. "She lives in Plumland, a place where she is the supreme dictator and does exactly what she wants to do."

"No, she's Plum the Merciless, an evil supervillain who terrorizes the planet Middle Schoolarus," Travis imagined.

"She's a giant pain in the neck, if you ask me," Mercedes said. "Whether she listens or not, I'm going to talk to her about laying off Shafir."

"I'll come with you," Daphne said. "I can't stand the way she yanks on the bit. Poor Shafir's just getting used to a bridle."

"That's how horses turn nasty," Mercedes agreed. "They're ridden by people like Plum until they grow to hate all people."

"She didn't cool Shafir down or anything," Daphne added. "If I hadn't stopped her she would have put her in her stall without even brushing her down, and she was about to give her a bucket of ice-cold water."

Taylor was reminded again of how all the horses Plum leased got sick or lame. "We can't let anything happen to Shafir. She's so friendly and playful. It would be horrible if she started hating people."

"Worse things than that could happen," Mercedes said darkly.

"Maybe we should tell her she can ride Shafir

hard during the event, but only then," Taylor suggested.

"It's too bad Eric can't tell her these things for us," Daphne said.

"He wouldn't," Travis commented. "He's Plum's cousin. What makes you think he's any better than she is?"

"He's not like Plum," Taylor defended Eric.

"Yeah?" Travis scoffed. "We'll see."

On Tuesday, in addition to her usual Wildwood cleaning and grooming chores, Taylor sorted through the box of old horseshoes Norman the farrier had donated. She was searching for shoes that weren't too bent for a horseshoe toss. Then she helped Travis hammer in the metal posts for the game.

The first part of Wednesday afternoon, Taylor told Alice, Dana, and Lois what to expect on Saturday. Taylor had never been to a horse show, but she had searched online. "What should she wear?" Alice asked.

"Well, what I read was that she should have on a riding jacket, breeches, and any color button-down shirt.

She doesn't have to wear riding gloves, but she could. You can buy a velvet cover to fancy up her helmet. Dana's hair won't fit in a bun, but maybe you could get it into a ponytail or pin it up at the sides."

Alice beamed affectionately at Dana, who sat atop Prince Albert, stroking his neck. "I can't wait to see how she looks in her riding gear!"

"She'll look adorable," Lois agreed. "I've rented the trailer for Friday evening so we can get it ready. That way there won't be any confusion in the morning. We need to leave by seven."

"Don't worry. I'll have Prince Albert all ready," Taylor assured her.

On Thursday, Taylor helped Mercedes and Daphne festoon the ranch with lines of red, blue, yellow, and white pennants. They climbed a ladder to hang the wires on which the multicolored triangles were attached from the main building to the big maple and back again to the building.

Travis and Eric climbed the maple and looped the pennants around the branches. Although Travis wasn't friendly to Eric, Taylor was glad to observe that he didn't insult him, either. He was controlling himself for the sake of Wildwood, which Taylor found very commendable.

By Friday, horses were starting to arrive in trailers of all sorts, ranging from small, one-horse trailers hitched to cars to monster trailers that were like buses. Mercedes, Daphne, Taylor, and even Travis and Mrs. LeFleur helped the owners get settled in their temporary stalls, which they rented for the night.

"We're going to move Pixie and Prince Albert into outdoor stalls," Mrs. LeFleur told Taylor. "We have to make way for paying customers."

"Won't they be cold?" Taylor asked, trying to disguise her dismay with a sensible question.

"There are horse blankets in the tack room, and it's only going down to the high forties tonight," Mrs. LeFleur said, and then hurried off to meet an incoming trailer.

Taylor stood there with her mouth open. Having to change Pixie and Albert's stalls had taken her by surprise.

"Don't look so horrified," Mercedes said. "They'll be okay out there. We had partially covered stalls like these back at our stable in Connecticut. None of our horses ever froze."

"How many horses did you have?" Taylor asked. It always sounded like Mercedes's family had their own herd.

"Lots," Mercedes confirmed.

"And you really think they'll be okay?"

"The hay gives off some heat, and so does the body temperature of the other horses. They're sheltered from the wind, and they have a roof. They'll be fine."

Despite Mercedes' words, Taylor still felt bad as she led Prince Albert and Pixie out of their inside stalls to the ones outside. "It's only for a night," she assured them. "Don't worry." She reminded herself that they had spent a week in Claire's front yard under a tarp and been fine, but that had been back in September when the weather was warmer.

There were horses in the paddock across from the outside stalls. Taylor knew things could be worse for Pixie and Prince Albert. Some horses didn't even have shelter. Others only had a run-in shed, a roof with only one side.

Turning, Taylor could see the paddock by the pasture, where Eric, Mercedes, and Daphne had set up an obstacle course, which would be the first event of Saturday morning.

Seeing the ranch so busy and filled with horses of every description helped Taylor envision Wildwood Stables the way it must have been back in the day when Mrs. LeFleur was a blue-ribbon jumper and Taylor's father came down here to ride. No wonder her father and Mr. Romano remembered it with such excitement. Experiencing the ranch like this gave Taylor a real glimpse into its vibrant past.

By the end of the day, all the horses were fed and watered. Taylor stood between the outdoor stalls and the paddock of grazing horses. She yawned and brushed her hair from her eyes as Daphne approached carrying a pail of water in her work-gloved hand. "We'd better go home, or we won't be good for anything tomorrow. I think we're all done," Daphne said.

A shrill neigh followed by pounding hoofbeats made Taylor and Daphne both turn toward the paddock. A big chestnut quarter horse with a star on its forehead was chasing a palomino with a white mane and white socks. The quarter horse gave chase until the palomino ran a good distance away. "What was that about?" Taylor wondered.

"They're establishing their pecking order," Daphne

explained. "They're like dogs or a lot of other animals that live in groups. They're vying to see who's at the top of the heap. That palomino was probably standing closer to the feeding trough than the big bay thought he should be."

"They're only staying overnight."

"They don't know that," Daphne reminded her. "So, what do you think? Should we go home? You don't want to ride back in the dark."

"Mrs. LeFleur will give me a lift if it gets too late. She's still doing stuff in the office. I want to get Prince Albert spruced up for tomorrow. Since he'll be outside, I don't want to wash him, but at least I can brush him down."

"Want me to show you how to braid his mane?" Daphne offered.

"Would you, really?" Taylor asked. She had always dreamed of having a horse with a braided mane. "Awesome!"

Chapter 16

On Saturday, Taylor rode her bike to Wildwood Stables at six-thirty in the morning. As she turned the corner from Wildwood Lane, the ranch seemed to glow with the pinks and golds of the first morning light. The festive pennants fluttered in the breeze. Occasionally, a horse sputtered while sleeping.

There would be so many people there that Taylor didn't feel it was safe to prop her bike against the maple as usual. Instead she got off and walked it to the main building. The activity of riding her bike had kept Taylor warm. Now that she was off it, she realized that it was a chilly October morning. In a week it would be Halloween, which meant daylight saving time would be ending any day now. The short days and long cold nights were about to begin.

Sliding open the front door, Taylor parked her bike in the tack room. Coming out to the center aisle, she felt how the body heat of all the horses warmed the building. Even though she was supposed to want more horse boarders, she hoped all of them didn't stay. Taylor wanted Prince Albert and Pixie to be able to return to their cozy stalls.

Taylor went around to the side stalls. Pixie was lying down in a nest of hay, sleeping. Prince Albert stood, already awake, watching the horses in the paddock across from him that were starting to move around. "How beautiful you look," Taylor praised him, impressed anew at the elegant French braid running down his back. His feed bucket was still half full, so she went to the old-fashioned hand pump in the back to get him some fresh water.

While she was pumping, Taylor heard cars arriving. The night before, just as Daphne and Taylor had finished Prince Albert's braid, Lois had arrived pulling a one-horse trailer hitched to a Jeep. They'd loaded all the tack and supplies they wanted to take. Now all there was left to do was to load Prince Albert and go.

Taylor let Prince Albert drink awhile and then let him

out of his stall. She was able to lead him simply by walking beside him with one hand on his side. As they passed Pixie's stall, she was awake and on her feet. "We'll be back later, Pixie," Taylor told her. "You're going to be giving pony rides today."

Pixie swung her head and neighed. Taylor knew she was demanding to come along with Prince Albert.

Prince Albert stopped, waiting for her.

"Come on, boy," Taylor said, nudging him forward. "She can't come this time." Prince Albert moved ahead several steps and then stopped as Pixie whinnied shrilly.

"Hi," Lois said, coming around the side of the building. She stopped when she noticed the distress on Taylor's face. "What's wrong?"

"Pixie's upset. I don't know if she's ever been apart from Prince Albert." Pixie turned in her stall and began kicking the door and neighing. Alarmed by the sounds, the horses in the paddock began whinnying uneasily. "I don't know what to do," Taylor admitted.

"I can't take her. It's just a one-horse trailer," Lois said.

Taylor heard a car door slam, and in the next moment Mrs. LeFleur came around the side of the building. "She won't let Prince Albert leave, will she?" she said. "I was worried this would be a problem."

"What should we do?" Taylor asked.

"Just leave, I'll handle it," Mrs. LeFleur said. "She'll settle down once Prince Albert's gone."

"But she'll be sad," Taylor objected.

"And then she'll be glad again when he returns. Pixie has to learn to be without Prince Albert sometimes. This is good for her." She went to Pixie's stall, clapping her hands sharply. "Stop that, Pixie! Stop it right now!"

For the first time, Taylor saw a flash of the horse-woman Mrs. LeFleur had once been.

"Take Prince Albert away. I can't calm her down until he's gone!"

Taylor worried about Pixie all the way to the field where the horse show was being held. When they drove into the parking lot it was already loaded with horse trailers. Some horses were still inside, while others were being walked around the grounds by their owners.

They found Alice and Dana parked on a grassy mound and pulled in beside Alice's car. Dana jiggled nervously in her new riding outfit — a dark blue riding jacket, tan breeches, a light blue button-down shirt, and short, shiny paddock boots. "You look terrific!" Taylor said to Dana as she walked toward her. "Just like a real horsewoman."

Taylor noticed that Dana's hands were fluttering like they had the first day she came to Wildwood. Instead of answering, the girl had a faraway look in her eyes. It made Taylor worry. "Prince Albert is here," she said to the girl. "Want to come see him?"

Dana didn't respond.

"She's very nervous," Alice said, sounding uneasy.

"I'll go get Prince Albert," Taylor offered, moving back toward the trailer.

Inside the paddock that had been set up on the field, Taylor stood beside Prince Albert with Dana in the saddle. They were in a row with four other riders on horseback with their horse handlers. All the riders were between the ages of six and eight. There was a boy who appeared to have Down syndrome. The girl beside Dana had a severely curved spine. The conditions the other riders had weren't apparent to Taylor. Mostly she was focused on Dana, relieved to see that her delicate hands were stroking Prince Albert's neck. She was no longer far away in her own world.

In front of them was a row of seated judges on a wooden platform. All around the paddock smiling parents, relatives, and friends watched.

"Walk forward," the center judge announced through a microphone.

Taylor nodded to Dana. The girl tapped Prince Albert with her heels, loosening her reins. "Chin up, shoulders back," Taylor whispered as Prince Albert stepped forward. Taylor wasn't leading him, but she was ready to grab the reins should anything go wrong.

The event involved halting, turning, walking some more, and halting again. Then the riders lined up and walked around in a line, following the inside perimeter of the paddock fence. "Walk at a steady pace," Taylor advised Dana. "Don't get ahead of the horse in front of you."

At the end of the event, all the riders won ribbons for participating. First, second, and third place ribbons were awarded for the horses. As they called the names of the horses, Taylor's eyes wandered around, gazing at the happy faces of the riders and their families. It was easy to see why Lois wanted to specialize in horse therapy. It had to feel wonderful to make so many people this happy.

"And first prize for best therapeutic horse goes to Prince Albert of Wildwood Stables!"

Taylor's head snapped forward. Had she heard the judge correctly? Taylor raised her eyebrows in a questioning expression and pointed to Prince Albert.

The judge laughed. "Yes, I said Prince Albert of Wildwood Stables," he repeated.

Glancing up at Dana, Taylor saw that her mouth was open and her eyes were like saucers.

"Come forward to collect Prince Albert's ribbon, please," the judge requested.

Taylor took the reins and led Prince Albert and Dana to the judge's platform. "Congratulations," the judge said, rising to hand Taylor the ribbon.

"Thank you so much," Taylor replied.

Leading Prince Albert out of the ring, Taylor knew she was beaming with pride and happiness. "You did it, Prince Albert!" she praised her horse, patting him robustly on his flank. "Good, good boy!"

Prince Albert whinnied happily, shaking his head.

Chapter 17

It was two in the afternoon when Lois pulled the horse trailer into Wildwood Lane. "Wait until Mrs. LeFleur hears the news," she said. "She's going to be so thrilled. This is huge."

"We're going to be incredibly busy if the entire County Therapeutic Riding Association wants to hold its lessons here at Wildwood," Taylor said.

"That's what the woman told me. She's going to call Mrs. LeFleur on Monday. It's going to mean a lot more clients for me, too," Lois said.

Not only had they won a blue ribbon, but Taylor and Prince Albert had won a huge account for Wildwood. She had convinced the woman in charge of the program that

Wildwood offered the best prices and facilities. Lois had agreed. Taylor knew they'd accomplished so much more than if they'd stayed for the games event.

Lois wasn't even to the bend in the road when they saw cars parked along Wildwood Lane. "The event is still going on, and it's packed," Lois observed.

As soon as they turned into the ranch, Taylor could hear the music wailing from the loudspeaker. She was amazed by Wildwood's transformation. There were people everywhere. A long line trailed out from where Norman was running his horseshoe toss. Travis's lemonade stand was also doing a brisk business. Beside him, Mercedes and Daphne could barely serve the donated pizza fast enough to their eager customers.

In the corral, Mrs. LeFleur was leading Pixie in a circle with an adorable four-year-old on her back. Whatever Mrs. LeFleur had done to calm the pony down had worked beautifully.

Eric met the Jeep as Lois parked it. "How did the games go?" Taylor asked him as she climbed out.

"Mostly other people we don't know won the ribbons, except Plum got a third in bandanna snatch," he reported.

That made sense to Taylor, knowing how much Shafir loved to play that game.

"Daphne won first in stalls, and Mercedes got a second in the obstacle course," Eric added. "Too bad you couldn't have competed. I bet you would have won something."

"Thanks, but we had a lot of fun. And we won a ribbon." She held it up to show him.

Eric raised his hand and Taylor slapped it.

"Look at this place," Taylor said as she headed to the back of the trailer to unload Prince Albert. "You really have to admit that Wildwood Stables is a great place."

"I see what you mean," Eric agreed. "It is pretty amazing."

Daphne and Mercedes noticed Taylor and waved. So did Travis.

Taylor waved her ribbon at them, grinning.

Instantly, her friends left their stations and ran toward her, cheering. As she opened the door to the trailer, they applauded Prince Albert and he neighed, sensing their praise.

Taylor's cheeks hurt from smiling. Wildwood Stables really was the best place in the world.

Come back to
WILDWOOD STABLES

Learning to Fly

Turn the page for a sneak peek!

Taylor Henry held Prince Albert's lead line casually in one hand as she walked the quarter horse down Wildwood Lane. The tree-lined country path leading in and out of Wildwood Stables was now vibrant with the rustling red, yellow, and orange hues of early autumn. Taylor could have easily ridden the black gelding on the dirt lane, but right then she preferred to be eye level with her horse.

They needed to have a serious talk.

"So, I know you love me. I love you just as much — more even! But it can't just be you and me. I wish it could," she told him.

Prince Albert neighed. Lately Taylor had noticed that whenever she spoke directly to Prince Albert he always made some noise in response. She loved that about him. It made her feel they were really communicating.

Taylor gazed into his soulful dark eyes and felt she heard him as clearly as if he'd actually replied aloud in words. He wanted to know why not. Why couldn't it just be Taylor and Prince Albert, without any other horses or riders?

"Because you have to be available for lessons and trail rides, that's why. And I need to work with the other horses." Taylor sighed in frustration. "It's part of our deal with Wildwood. Don't pretend you don't know all this. We've been through it a zillion times already!"

At this point Taylor was sure Prince Albert was simply being stubborn. It was mid-October, and he'd been living at the stable since the end of August. By now he had to understand that he couldn't be a one-girl horse.

Taylor had helped rescue him and his best pal, a cream Shetland pony named Pixie, when they'd been abandoned by their owners. Against all odds, she'd even found them a good home here at Wildwood Stables. But the ranch could only afford to keep Prince Albert if he was a working trail and school horse. And, so far, he had not been at all cooperative.

"Sure, I know you've let Dana ride you," Taylor acknowledged. Dana was a seven-year-old girl with autism who had horse therapy sessions at the stable once a week. She would only work with Prince Albert, and to everyone's surprise, he allowed her on his back. They had even won a ribbon at a recent Rotary Club horse competition for kids with disabilities.

"And it's really great that you let her on; it's meant so much to her," Taylor continued. "But you have to do more. Being a two-girl horse is still not enough. Okay?"

A black SUV swung in very quickly from Quail Ridge Road at the end of the lane. It zoomed toward Taylor and Prince Albert as though the driver was completely unaware that a slim thirteen-year-old girl with long brown hair and a large black horse were standing in the path.

Startled by the car's speed, Taylor dropped the lead line and jumped back. Prince Albert reared in fright, neighing shrilly as his front two legs rose from the ground, kicking the air.

The glamorous blonde woman at the wheel of the SUV careened into a rapid curve to avoid the frightened horse in her path, but made no effort to slow down. Beside the woman, a slim girl Taylor's age, also a blonde, watched the scene with unmistakable annoyance etched on her face.

Staggering backward, Taylor recognized the girl and the car just as the heel of her brown riding boot hit a tree root. Taylor fell on her butt, sending rockets of pain up her spine. As she scrambled to her feet, she couldn't stop to feel her injury, or even her fury at Plum Mason and her reckless mother.

Her entire attention was on Prince Albert, who was galloping in wild panic toward Quail Ridge Road.

Panting hard, heart thundering in her chest, Taylor raced down Wildwood Lane onto steep and curving Quail Ridge Road. Fast as she was running, it seemed to take forever to get there.

Taylor checked the field to her left. Some of Wildwood's other horses had been turned out and grazed there — but no Prince Albert.

Pivoting to her right, Taylor froze.

"Oh, no!" she shouted.

Up the hill, Prince Albert stood in the middle of the road, wide-eyed and bewildered. He was standing directly in the middle of a blind curve in the road. If a car came around the bend now, the driver would never see him in time to stop.

"Prince Albert! Prince Albert!" Taylor shouted in her most commanding tone.

Prince Albert swung his head around to her. His ears were back and flattened, a sign of his anxiety.

Taylor clapped her hands sharply. "Walk on! Move, Prince Albert! Now! Move to the other side! Get off the road!"

Prince Albert usually obeyed commands well. Why wasn't he moving?

His nostrils flared and his eyes were wide. He stood frozen in terrified confusion.

Clicking to the frightened horse, Taylor hurried up the hill toward him, deciding on another approach. "Come to me, boy. Come on." She worked to disguise the urgent fear in her voice, hoping he would calm down enough to respond.

It was no use! He wasn't budging.

"Move!" Taylor shouted, full blast, clenching her fists as her cheeks reddened with the strain. Maybe she could at least startle him off the road.

At the sound of her agitated tone, Prince Albert whinnied and turned his body toward Taylor. As he moved, a large white car came into view, coming fast.

Prince Albert screamed as he reared high onto his back legs.

The car's horn blared, and then came the sickening sound of crunching metal.

Taylor was only dimly aware of her own anguished voice shouting.

"No! No! No!"

Daring to Dream

Taylor Henry loves horses, but her single mom can't afford riding lessons, much less a horse. So when she discovers an abandoned gelding and pony, Taylor is happy just to be around them.

But the rescued animals have nowhere to go, and Taylor is running out of time to find them a good home. Could the empty old barn on Wildwood Lane be the answer? And could Taylor's wildest dream—of a horse to call her own—finally be coming true?

Playing for Keeps

Taylor Henry thinks Wildwood Stables is perfect—even if it needs repair and a lot more money, it's become a home to her and her new horse, Prince Albert. And as soon as Taylor trains Prince Albert to give lessons, Wildwood will be in business!

But the gelding refuses to let anyone ride him except Taylor. Can she convince Prince Albert to earn his keep? Or will Taylor need the help of her worst enemy to save her beloved new home?

Read them all!

CANDY APPLE BOOKS
Read them all!